A Wife

for

Hamilton

WENDY MAY ANDREWS

CR&D

Sparrow Ink
www.sparrowdeck.com

ISBN - 978-1-989634-53-0

www.wendymayandrews.com

Marry in haste, repent at leisure...

Sadie Fitzsimmons must choose between total destitution and marriage by proxy with someone she's never met.

When Sadie steps off the train to meet her new husband for the first time, life in Nebraska is not at all what she had expected. Torn between honoring the vows she spoke to a stranger, and her desire to be free of all obligations, Sadie must face the consequences of her choices.

Hamilton Foster had worked hard for his successes. All that was missing from his perfect life was a family of his own. Sending home to Boston for a wife seemed like a good idea until she arrived and she was too pretty to be trusted.

Follow along to see if these two can find their happily ever after.

Dedication

Honesty and communication are themes
running through this book. I believe strongly
in both of these, especially in any relationship.
I dedicate this book to everyone struggling
with either or both. You will enjoy watching
Sadie and Hamilton learn.

Acknowledgements

My books wouldn't happen without the support of my fabulous hubby. He helps in every way imaginable. I'm blessed to have my own real-life hero.

My parents are my biggest fans, supporting and cheering for me every step of the way. I wouldn't have life without them, nor would I enjoy it nearly as much.

My beta readers – Marlene, Suzanne, Monique, Alfred, and Christina – help me immeasurably. Their help with the story as well as care and compassion for the author are a blessing.

Thanks to *GermanCreative* for this beautiful cover.

Julie Sherwood's edits are amazing and she is a delight to work with. Any remaining errors are the author's.

Chapter One

The two men leaning against the faded clapboard wall watched the passengers disembarking from the train with interest. Hamilton Foster's interest was somewhat more intense than that of his foreman, whose interest seemed more amused than involved.

"Do you think that's her?" Herman asked, indicating the young woman just stepping down from the train with the thrust of his chin.

"No," Hamilton's answer was immediate and terse.

"How can you be sure? I thought you said your friend didn't send any pictures."

"I haven't seen an image of her, but I'm certain that is not my wife. I was very specific in the request that my wife be homely. That woman is ridiculously pretty, so she is surely not Mrs. Foster."

The chuckle with which Herman answered his statement caused Hamilton to scowl more fiercely.

"As long as you're sure, Foster, then we'll keep waiting."

Hamilton glared at the man for his flippant tone but didn't move from his slouch in the growing shade of the building. He couldn't imagine what was taking his bride so long to get off the train. It would seem the girl wasn't eager to meet him. What a bother.

After a futile ten minutes of standing there with no other passengers getting down from the train, Hamilton shook his head. "She must have missed her last connection," he said, trying to keep the disgust from his voice. It wouldn't do to speak ill of his wife in front of any of his men, even if it was the stupidest thing to do. He thought he had emphasized he didn't want a dull-witted woman as his wife. He stood straight and was about to head toward the wagon when Herman interrupted his movement.

"Don't you suppose we ought to ask that woman if she's met your bride?"

"Why would you assume they would have met?"

Herman shrugged. "Women are a scarcity. I would imagine any heading West would have introduced themselves."

Hamilton scowled but nodded, turning back toward the train platform without another word.

"Excuse me, ma'am, might I have a word?"

Hamilton thought he had braced himself for the impact of her beauty, but he was mistaken. He felt the reaction all the way down to his heels as they rocked backward away from the vision before him.

"Yes?" she asked in a soft, questioning, timid voice.

"We're looking for Sadie Foster. She was travelling West from Boston. Is there any chance you might have encountered her on your journey?"

The woman blinked at him as a frown wrinkled her brow.

"I'm Sadie," she answered simply.

Hamilton stared at her and had to fight to stifle a curse, turning his glare from the woman to his supposed friend who was doing a poor job of hiding his laughter. The woman looked puzzled and nervous.

"Are you Mr. Foster? Did Mr. Fredericksburg not describe me to you? He bade me to remember to wear my hat so you would recognize me."

Hamilton could tell that he was scaring the girl, so he tried to clamp down on the anger that was simmering inside him. It would not do to allow it to boil over and scorch his wife, no matter how angry he might be. It wasn't her fault Fredericksburg had lied. Or perhaps it was. Hamilton wasn't to know for sure.

"He did write about the hat. I just wouldn't have described that little thing as a hat. It's not going to provide you much protection in these parts."

As he spoke, her hand flew to her head, and she blushed as though she were guilty of something, making Hamilton's frown deepen.

"It's true that it's not at all practical, but Mr. Fredericksburg said you'd have an easier time finding me if I wore it."

Herman snorted behind him, no longer bothering to conceal his laughter. The discomfort and embarrassment covering his wife's face made Hamilton turn and shove his foreman.

"Cut it out, Herman," he growled. It didn't seem to help his wife. She looked all the more uncomfortable as her wide eyes gazed up at him, filling with fear.

In that moment, Hamilton deeply regretted the decision he had made to send for a wife. Marrying a stranger had clearly been a mistake. He didn't know how to deal with taking responsibility for a woman in the first place, but especially not one he didn't even know. It had seemed like a good idea at the time, but Hamilton was beginning to question the wisdom of his rash actions. But they were already married, had been legally committed by proxy, before the girl even got on the westbound train.

"You *are* Mr. Foster, are you not?" the girl asked, her nervous hands fluttering as she gazed up at him. She was a tiny little thing, he thought, wondering how she would be able to manage life on the frontier.

"I am," he finally answered her. "Where are your trunks? We ought to get going." Hamilton was none too happy about the attention his beautiful wife was drawing. Herman hadn't been exaggerating when he said women were a scarcity. And a beautiful woman was nearly as rare as some mythological creature. This one would be a draw that he'd have to protect. It was a complication he could ill afford. A small part of him wanted to put her on the next train back to Boston, but that would be cowardly and deceitful. He had committed himself by means of the proxy papers he had signed. He would have to honor his word. But he didn't have to like it. His scowl deepened.

"Over there." Her hand and voice shook as she pointed toward the two small bags on the platform. Hamilton looked at her with disapproval.

"Will we have to come to meet the train another day for the rest of your things?"

"What were you expecting me to bring with me? This is all I have."

Hamilton couldn't name all the emotions that flitted across her face, but he was fairly certain she was embarrassed and angry. He couldn't, for the life of him, understand why.

"I just expected you'd have brought more with you for such a big move," he tried to explain himself, although he was uncomfortable with the need to do so.

The girl merely nodded and shrugged, not providing any further information. Hamilton was surprised by her reticence. He had never met a woman who didn't chatter. Not that he had met many women in the past several years. As Herman had said, women were scarce in the West. But small, pretty women from Boston – he had known plenty of those in the past, and they had been chatterboxes, every last one of them.

Gritting his teeth, Hamilton stalked over to the bags and tucked one under each arm while he listened to his foreman attempt to charm his wife.

"I'm Herman, Mrs. Foster, it's a pleasure to meet you."

He couldn't hear a response, but that might have been just because she was soft spoken.

"Don't mind Foster, he's just surly."

Hamilton wanted to put his fist through his friend's face to relieve his tension. He threw the bags in the wagon instead then climbed up onto the bench and waited for Herman to hand up his wife. The small woman now looked terrified. But she was still beautiful. Hamilton wanted to curse. She was supposed to be homely. How was he going to handle having a pretty woman as his wife?

~~~

Sadie swallowed her misgivings and allowed the men to squish her between them. She would rather be anywhere but there. The man who was her husband had barely done anything but glower and growl at her but still, her ridiculous heart had sped up whenever she caught a glimpse of him.

Her palms felt sweaty, and her stomach fluttered uncomfortably. Maybe she was coming down with some dreadful disease. She never should have agreed to marry a stranger and move to the literal ends of the earth. Jane had tried to help her see that it was a better choice than whatever Oscar had to offer her.

Just the thought of Oscar sent a shiver up Sadie's spine. She stifled a sigh. Maybe she really was coming down with some deadly disease. Perhaps death would be better than the great unknown yawning before her. Marriage to this stranger had saved her from Oscar, but could she really trust whatever future this frowning stranger had to offer her? At that moment, it didn't matter that a friend of a friend had vouched for him. That was the flimsiest of references, Sadie now realized.

Staring out around her, Sadie still couldn't get over how very flat it all was. And as soon as they had left the small village where the train station was, it seemed like they were the only living creatures around. At least the only humans. She had spotted various creatures in the distance or startled off the roadway in front of them as they passed swiftly through the landscape, pulled by the very large horses.

While she normally enjoyed silence, since there was often so little of it, now the fact that neither man was speaking grated on her nerves. Sadie thought to fill the silence but hadn't a clue where to start.

She cleared her throat before speaking, which brought the gaze of both men toward her, making her falter. But when her raised eyebrows didn't prompt either of them into speech, Sadie forced herself to begin talking.

"Do we have very far to go?"

Mr. Foster was holding the reins in a fashion that looked like he was skilled in the matter. Sadie had next to no experience in such things, but it seemed to her that he did. He divided his attention between her and the horses.

"We live about three hours from town," he finally answered as his frown returned. "I probably should have asked if you needed to make any purchases before we left. Have you eaten?"

His frown was discouraging, but Sadie managed not to falter. She was relieved to hear that they had such a short distance to travel. She had actually feared they might have to spend the night on the trail. She had accepted that as a possibility after talking with people on the long train ride West.

"I'm fine, thank you."

She was also lying. She was extremely intimidated by the situation she found herself in. Sandwiched in between the two large men, she was left to wonder why her new husband had brought the other man with him. Perhaps he had thought he would be bored on the three-hour drive to collect her. But they didn't seem to be on particularly good terms with each other, barely exchanging a word since she had joined them.

Sadie chastised herself for her stupidity. She should have insisted on having more information about the man who was now her husband. She had committed her future to a stranger. And now she had to live with the consequences. Namely, fear and uncertainty.

Very well, Sadie, pull it together, she admonished herself. You've lived through challenges in the past. You'll live through this one as well. Or you won't, she thought with the threat of hysterical laughter as all her fears piled on top of one another. Refusing to succumb to her fears and give in to a fit of hysterics, Sadie tried for more conversation.

"Do you live nearby, Mr. Herman?"

The man on her left chuckled. "Nearby to you, do you mean, Mrs. Foster?"

Sadie nodded, but the action was tentative.

"That I do, ma'am. I'm your husband's foreman, so I live right next door to you."

Not even sure why she had asked, Sadie was undecided if she were relieved with this information or not. She nodded again.

"Do you have many other neighbors?"

The driver merely grunted in response, prompting another chuckle from the foreman. "I suppose it depends on your definition of neighbor."

It wasn't much of an answer; Sadie couldn't stop her sigh. Herman laughed again. "Foster has a great deal of land, ma'am, so neighboring properties are a fair distance away. But the men live on the property, and there's a small village less than an hour away with plenty of people. In between Foster's and the village there are a few other homesteads. It's not exactly Boston, but if you're looking for company, you will be able to find it."

Sadie turned back to watching the road. From the side of her gaze, she could see Mr. Foster's profile. It would be a while before she could think of him as her husband, she was sure. He was handsome in a stark kind of way with a wide, firm chin and cheekbones that were slashes in his sun burnished face. The tanned hue to his face seemed to enhance the blueness of his eyes. Sadie normally liked blue eyes, but on Mr. Foster they seemed to only contribute to the sense that he was cold and hard. With all that, it was rather ridiculous that Sadie found herself wanting to gaze at him. She would normally consider herself to be a sensible woman, but she had clearly become addled somewhere along the way, as she had absolutely no intention of finding the man appealing. He was a means to an end.

But why would such a good looking, obviously successful financially, man still be single, in need of arranging a bride by proxy? It made no sense to Sadie, even if you factored in the shortage of women in the West. There might not be as many as in the East, but surely there were *some*! And if not, the trains that had brought Sadie here ran in both directions. Surely, the man could have done some travelling and found a wife for himself. She had good reason to be a little skeptical. She was no longer quick to offer her trust. In this particular case, despite the fact that she was married to the man, there was no way she could trust him.

Sadie had been expecting a rather off-putting man from a physical perspective. She had been wrong on that front, but his grouchy demeanor was still off-putting, even if he was pleasant to look at. Perhaps that was why he had needed a bride by proxy. No woman would have him after meeting him in person. The thought made her smile slightly. Perhaps it wasn't such a mismatch after all. At first glance, Mr. Foster seemed like a matrimonial prize. But clearly, there were reasons for his single state. It was a strangely comforting thought for Sadie. She could never give him her heart, and if she could find a way out of the marriage eventually, she would happily take it, but for now, she would do her best to uphold her end of their bargain.

Just nobody better expect her to love the man. She'd seen the damage love could do. Look at what she went through loving and losing her entire family. No, she would be loyal to Mr. Foster for as long as he was her husband, and do her best to fill whatever role he expected of her, but she would never give him her heart. It didn't matter if he was handsome as the devil. Even if he turned out not to be the surly bear he appeared to be, she added as a reminder to her heart, just to cover all the possible aspects of the matter.

Turning her attention once more to the road ahead, Sadie tried to ignore the gnawing ache in her stomach. Some of it was nerves, but mostly it was because she had run out of money and had thus not eaten since the previous morning. Feeling the churning inside, Sadie only hoped it didn't actually growl out loud. She didn't think she could bear the mortification. She had thought she had packed enough food for the journey, but there had been delays and there had been other hungry passengers she just couldn't ignore. After sharing a little of her provisions and sending the telegraph to Mr. Foster as Mr. Fredericksburg had instructed, she had nothing left. Sadie blocked the unwelcome thoughts and sensations from her mind. It wasn't the first time she had experienced hunger pangs; she doubted it would be the last. Lamenting would accomplish nothing.

But then a wild growl erupted from her middle, and Sadie wanted to leap from the wagon and disappear. No way would the handsome man consider her a proper wife if she couldn't even control the unwelcome sounds that a body makes.

"I thought you said you were fine." He frowned down from his great height beside her. Sadie kept her gaze directly between the two ears of the giant horse on the right.

"I am, thank you again for asking," she replied, despite the fierce blush she could feel suffusing her entire being.

"Well, I know that sound came from you, so unless you have some strange way of communicating that I've never heard tell of, you are hungry. When is the last time you ate?"

"I don't really see how that's any of your concern, Mr. Foster."

"I beg your pardon?"

Sadie's flush deepened, but she still didn't look at either man. Out of the corner of her eye, she could see Herman reaching under the seat.

"I'm feeling a tinge peckish myself. It's a good thing I brought this bag of sandwiches for us, isn't it? Would you like one, Foster?"

He didn't even bother asking her, just handed one to Sadie without comment.

Mr. Foster didn't speak further, but Sadie felt his gaze burning into the side of her head. She made every effort to ignore him while she concentrated on not devouring the sandwich like the wild animal she had sounded when her stomach growled.

The handsome man seemed to simmer with anger. Sadie couldn't fathom what the man had to be angry about. It was rude of him to ask her about her hunger, surely he must realize that. Her refusal to answer was no reason for him to be angry. And if it was her hunger that angered him, well that was completely ridiculous, too, because it wasn't really his problem. And now it was taken care of. Sadie ought to thank Herman, but she couldn't muster up the gumption to speak at the moment.

Another, worse, thought occurred to Sadie. What if Mr. Foster was just always angry? That would be a terrible outcome to all these arrangements. The Fredericksburgs had spoken highly of him. Not that they had known him personally, but they said he came highly recommended from good friends of theirs. Sadie now realized that was the slimmest of all possible recommendations. She ought to have stayed in Boston and tried to sort out the situation with Oscar herself. Surely, if she had persisted in looking a little bit harder, she would have eventually found a position that would have paid enough to get the awful man to leave her alone.

Sadie continued to stare at the horses' ears, deep in thought. Focusing on the what ifs wasn't going to get her anywhere. She had signed the documents Jane's husband had drawn up for her. Mr. Foster was her husband. She had used her own free will and made the vow. She owed it to everyone to keep her word. Yes, she should have thought it through a little more before she signed and got on the train, but at the time, it felt like a welcome respite from the pressure she had been under from that wretch Oscar.

It was amazing what a little break from stress will do. Ten days out of her hovel of an apartment, and she was already changing her mind about decisions she had made. She was being foolish, and it had to stop.

Lifting her chin, Sadie decided to face her situation head on.

"I apologize, sir. I was hungry and wretched and not feeling very polite. While I think it was a little impertinent of you to ask me about it, I shouldn't have been rude in return. I was hungry as I had run out of funds and hadn't yet eaten today." Sadie turned to Herman, who was looking on with unmasked interest. "Thank you so much for being prepared to alleviate all our hunger. You were right to come prepared. Your drive would have necessitated a meal at some point. I'm glad you planned enough for me to have some, too."

Much to her delighted surprise, Herman's ears turned pink, as though her thanks embarrassed him. "It was barely anything, ma'am. I'm sorry it was so necessary for you, but I'm glad to be of service." He even lifted his head and gave her a slight bow. Mr. Foster, on the other hand, looked as though he were ready to explode with anger.

"What happened to the money Fred was to give you to make all your arrangements? Surely, you didn't bring enough luggage to have spent it all on fripperies."

Sadie wished she had kept silent.

"I had to buy my train ticket, for one thing. I also had some pressing obligations that needed to be cared for before I was free to leave. There were also even less fortunate souls on the train than me."

"And you felt obliged to give my money to them?"

"Mr. Fredericksburg led me to understand that it was, in fact, my money, sir." She answered with quiet dignity, silencing the man at her side. But he continued to glower.

Chapter Two

They continued the journey in silence. Sadie surmised that if she could observe them, they most likely looked humorous. From her peripheral vision, she could see that Mr. Foster was frowning and angry looking. On her other side, Herman appeared inordinately pleased, although she had no idea why he would look so delighted. Perhaps he was just one of those perpetually happy people, she thought with a mental shrug. Sadie was certain that her face was probably a mix of the two.

Despite the very large question marks looming in front of her, Sadie was thrilled to be gone from Boston. She was no longer within Oscar's reach. Her debts were paid. She was safe. Despite how surly her husband seemed, he had been vouched for by people she trusted. Or at least as far as she trusted anyone these days. Even though the man seemed like a cranky bear, she didn't have any reason to feel that he was a threat to her, and his large, looming size actually filled her with a sense of security. He might be growly about it, but he had wanted her to be safe and fed. It warmed her heart more than she was comfortable to admit.

Shoving the unwelcome thoughts from her mind, Sadie watched with interest as they drove through a very small village. This was where Herman had said she could find company if she needed. At this point in time,

Sadie wanted to curl up in a room and be alone for the next year or two, but she doubted she would ever have that luxury. Instead, she would content herself with not seeking company. At least for a time. But it was still good to know there was somewhere to make necessary purchases, she acknowledged as they left the village behind after slowing enough to allow the men to nod at the shopkeeper of the mercantile.

Before she had time for her mind to wander too far, they were slowing again and turning onto a road that looked very similar to the road they were already travelling. But then she saw, off in the distance, a collection of buildings including a very appealing house. Her heart quickened. *Was that her new home?* Sadie contained her excitement and didn't bounce in the seat, but she couldn't keep her eyes off the house as they drove steadily toward it.

It rose up from the cluster of buildings on a small knoll, two stories of gently aging clapboard planks. Somehow, it felt to Sadie as though the house were calling to her. As though it were already her home. As though she had lived there for years and had just somehow forgotten it. It made her feel slightly irrational to be experiencing the sensation, but there was no arguing with how she felt. The house seemed to welcome her.

Too bad Sadie was hoping for a way out of her marriage.

But for the time being, she was going to enjoy the sensation. She had experienced so little enjoyment in the recent past. Sadie was certain there must have been times that she had enjoyed herself in the far off past. Her childhood had been sufficiently carefree, filled with childish giggles and easily procured treats. But the recent years so overshadowed all else that it was hard to remember she had ever not been careworn.

This house didn't appear careworn. It didn't even appear all that old, despite the aging clapboard. Sadie rather supposed that in the strong sun, that could happen in a matter of months or maybe a year or two. She thrilled as they came through a copse of trees, and she gained a different perspective of the house. Dormer windows! Her very favorite. And there were two. She would never want to leave the house now. She shook away the unwelcome thought. One always did what one must, she reminded herself fiercely before returning to chronicling all the details of the homestead that was steadily rising up before her.

As Herman had said, there were fields spreading out in all directions, as far as the eye could see. Nearby to the house there were several outbuildings, including what looked like several small houses. She wondered if that was where Herman and some of the other workers lived. Perhaps, too, there were hens and such. Sadie, having lived her entire life within the confines of Boston, wasn't completely certain what all one would find on a homestead but she knew, even in the city, many raised chickens and hens. Her family even had before they'd been forced to move into the shared accommodations after her father had taken ill.

One more thought to shake off, Sadie reminded herself and turned her attention to the vista before her once more. Horses and cows, she could now see, dotted the rolling hills spreading out from the barn. Even some sheep and goats. She wasn't completely certain how it was accomplished, but she was certain the sheep wool would be removed and they could make clothing from it. The thought of warm woolen socks and mitts filled her with another wave of security that she made an effort to ignore. She didn't need to find her sense of security from such external things, she reminded herself fiercely. She had managed just fine without a strong man to care and provide for her.

Had you really, though, her conscience prodded her. Give the man his due. You wouldn't have been free of your debt without Mr. Foster. And you wouldn't be more than half a country away from Oscar, either. You owe him more than secret schemes to get away. You owe him your loyalty, at least for a time.

Sadie knitted her lips together in a line, acknowledging the truth of her inner thoughts. She owed Foster more than he knew. She would do her best to be a good wife for as long as he needed. She had taken vows before God and the Fredericksburgs.

She finally turned toward the frowning man at her side. "It's quite a large homestead, isn't it, Mr. Foster?"

~~~

Hamilton gazed down at the small woman at his side. He was surprised that she had finally addressed him directly, voluntarily. It had seemed as though she were avoiding him as much as was possible while crammed against him on the narrow seat. The wagon had seemed quite spacious while he and Herman had driven to the train station, but he had been constantly aware of the pretty creature as she sat stiffly beside him ever since she had been handed up into the wagon. Even the sound of her voice was delightful, making Hamilton want to curse. He was well aware that he was being beastly. It was probably beyond ridiculous to be angry to find out his wife was pretty. But he had thought he had been very clear with Fred. He did not want a pretty wife.

Dragging his thoughts back toward her question, as he felt her questioning gaze still rested on his face, Hamilton wasn't sure exactly how to answer.

"Yes," he finally answered, smiling to hear the note of pride in his tone.

"Have you lived here long?"

"Didn't Fred tell you?" It wasn't that he didn't want to tell her, it just felt too much like bragging if he told her himself. But once again he had embarrassed her, he could see by the color flooding her cheeks.

"He was too busy explaining the legalities of the situation to go into very many details about you, sir." She stammered out the reply.

"Did he tell you anything?"

She cleared her throat with a delicate cough. If Hamilton could correctly read her expression, she was wishing she hadn't raised any subject with him. He wished he had just been able to answer her question directly. He was being a wretch toward her. And she was probably exhausted from more than a week of travel, besides being such a tiny little thing the next big gust of wind might blow her off the wagon seat if she weren't wedged in between the two men. He didn't know if she was going to finally answer. She surprised him.

"Mr. Fredericksburg told me you left Boston for California a little over ten years ago. But I don't think he mentioned how long you've been here. Did you stop here on your way to California and decide to settle here?"

"There were no trains this far when I came West. But yes, when I was passing through, I knew I wanted to own a piece of this beautiful land. Thankfully, the government makes it easy, since I've never spoken or raised arms against this nation. It was quite a simple thing to place a claim to the land. I got my first claim as I was passing through. I had five years to start developing the land. When I came back, I expanded my claim with ranching. So yes, you could say it's quite a sizeable homestead."

She was watching him expectantly as though she were hoping for more information. He almost grunted.

"With the arrival of the trains, more people are arriving every week, so I'm glad I laid my claim to so much land when I had the opportunity."

"You would prefer not to have too many neighbors?"

He shrugged.

"I just don't like the idea of being limited. I now have more land than I have any use for, but maybe I'll need it later. If all the parcels around me are already claimed, I'll be mad as a hornet."

This surprised a tinkle of laughter out of the tiny creature.

"You do have a way with words."

"And besides, if we have any hopes of building a dynasty here, we need room to grow."

"A dynasty?" Now she sounded even more hesitant than she had when he had been growly.

"For our children and grandchildren," he explained as her color rose once more.

"I don't think I'm ready to entertain the idea of dynasties just yet, sir," she replied, her tone prim and strained, making Herman smirk. Hamilton had to fight the urge to show him the business end of a fist.

Hamilton felt as though his ears were heating up, and he wasn't sure if it was from embarrassment or anger, but he felt compelled to reassure the woman, despite his own discomfort.

"Not immediately, of course, but eventually, children would be an expected result of our vows, don't you think?"

She still didn't turn back toward him, keeping her head bowed and her eyes downcast, but he was fairly certain she gave a small bob of her head in agreement.

Hamilton didn't want to leave the conversation on such an awkward note, so he tried to introduce another topic.

"Do you think you'll be uncomfortable so far out in the wilderness?"

This finally brought her head back up, and she looked at him with a puzzled frown.

"Is this wilderness, sir? I rather thought it looked somewhat civilized. At least more so than some of the places I could see from the train as we travelled here. The gently rolling hills are far less intimidating than some of the mountainous regions the train went through closer to Boston. And some that I spoke with on the train said that the further West one goes, it gets even rockier. So I think this is rather nice."

"True, but we are a week's journey from the big cities you're used to."

Hamilton couldn't read her expression as she gazed at him, barely blinking. She finally spoke. "Some might consider that to be a very good thing, sir." She paused for a moment with a slight frown before continuing. "So to answer your question, no, I don't think I'll be uncomfortable, at least not from the distance. It would seem from the size of your property and buildings, there is plenty of space to make oneself comfortable in. I'm looking forward to not feeling squashed."

"I apologize about the wagon, ma'am," Hamilton began, feeling chastised. "I hadn't thought you would have so little luggage. If I had realized, I would have brought a conveyance that allowed more room for people."

His brows arched in surprise as she once more giggled.

"Do not trouble yourself, sir, I wasn't meaning right now." She gestured toward the fields as she said, "After a lifetime of living in a rapidly expanding city and then more than a week on the train, I'm looking forward to not living piled on top of other people."

"Did you live in an apartment, then, rather than a house?"

"Yes," she answered simply.

"Is that why you've been staring at my house ever since it came into view?"

Her smile didn't look embarrassed, Hamilton was relieved to see. Even though he wasn't too happy with Fred's choice of such a pretty woman for him, he was very glad to note that she was a cheerful sort.

"Yes, I was hoping that was your house. It is delightful. So big and spacious. And those dormer windows look so inviting. That house looks as though it was built for comfort, not to impress or intimidate."

"Well, you're right about that. It would be ridiculous to build a house way out here with the intention of impressing anyone other than myself. Who's going to see it?"

She again laughed shortly. "So true. But sometimes people dream big and feel the need to fulfill it whether it makes sense or not."

Hamilton pondered her words, wondering what sort of dreams she might have but feeling it would be much too intrusive to ask her about them just yet. She hadn't appreciated his question about her hunger; she wasn't likely to want to tell him about her dreams. They had just met, after all, even if they were already wed. Not that he was all that interested in what was going on inside her head, he reminded himself. He couldn't be bothered with a pretty woman. He needed to ignore the inclination to listen to her and especially his misguided impulse to gaze at her. Yes, he had to keep an eye on her, but that was only to make sure she wasn't getting up to nonsense. If she was going to bear his name, he needed to ensure she didn't sully it in any way.

Feeling his face tightening, Hamilton turned his gaze back toward the house. Despite his reservations about her, he had been thrilled to witness her interest in his home.

"Did you always live in an apartment?" he surprised himself by asking.

"Since my father got sick and couldn't work as hard as he once had."

"How old were you when that happened?"

"I was seven years old."

"Barely out of infancy, then," he commented. "It's the worst age to leave a house behind. Children should have space to run and play."

The woman lifted one shoulder in what he supposed was meant to look as though she didn't care overly much, but Hamilton suspected she wasn't nearly as care free as she would like him to think. She wouldn't have been looking at his house with such anticipation if she didn't care that she had been forced out of her childhood home.

"There was plenty of space to run and play in the streets," she finally commented, "but there wasn't much time for playing once my father died."

"I'm sorry for your loss," Hamilton answered instinctively.

Her eyes were shiny with unshed tears when she glanced briefly at him before she quickly lowered her head back down to her contemplation of the horses.

"Did you think a woman with family and prospects would agree to marry a stranger without ever having met him?" She didn't sound confrontational, merely curious.

Hamilton felt his color rising once again when he heard the pride in his tone as he answered her. "I could be considered quite an eligible catch for a young woman, regardless of her background."

Herman snorted beside them, reminding them of his presence.

"Do you have something to add, Herman?" Hamilton nearly growled.

"Not a thing, Boss, except that I'm glad I don't have to listen to this much longer." Herman's cheerful tone set Hamilton's teeth on edge but before he could respond, Herman had jumped over the side of the wagon before Hamilton had even begun to pull the horses to a standstill in front of the barn.

"I'll take care of these two if you want to show your missus around your empire."

Hamilton would have shown the other man exactly what he thought of his impudence except the small woman at his side allowed another silvery tinkle of her laughter to float by on the breeze.

He felt an immediate physical reaction. HIs gut tightened with a curious mixture of awareness and rejection. Yes, he was attracted to her, but he had absolutely no wish to be. Hamilton held back his groan of frustration. He had an exceedingly awkward future ahead of him.

As he showed her around the near property - the barn, small animal pens, chicken coop, the ranch hands' housing, and finally his own house - he marveled over her varied reactions. It was more than obvious she had never been outside the city before. She hadn't even known how to collect eggs. But she had been a very quick study. After he had shown her twice, she had quickly collected a basketful. It had been cute to watch her timidly approaching the roosts but then nearly crowing with delight when she found what she was searching for.

"Do you suppose they're disappointed?" she had asked with a worried frown as they moved on toward the rest of the tour.

"Who?" Surely she couldn't be asking about the hens.

"The chickens. That their eggs are gone. This means they won't be able to have any babies, right?"

Hamilton stared at her, barely preventing his chin from dropping open.

"First of all, the ones laying the eggs are called hens. And they are not emotionally invested in their eggs, so you needn't worry." He tried to keep any sarcasm out of his tone.

When her expression of concern wasn't completely alleviated, Hamilton continued to explain.

"We don't keep the rooster together with all the hens. We would be overrun with chicks if we did so. We keep the hens for egg production and for eating. But this is only for our personal use, not for business. So, we need to keep it under control. If you didn't collect those eggs, they would be useless to the hens. They could sit on them forever. No chicks would be coming out of them."

Her rapt stare of concentration made Hamilton slightly uncomfortable.

"Do you understand what I'm talking about?" A horrid thought crossed his mind. "Do you understand how chicks are produced? And also all offspring, by extension?"

Color splashed across her face, and she looked as though she wished to be anywhere but before him in that moment, but she gave a slight nod. "Because the rooster isn't present with these chickens, I mean, hens, then no chicks will be produced from the eggs. And similar for humans and all other reproducing creatures, I suppose."

"Yes, exactly." Hamilton fervently wished he hadn't raised the topic, but it needed to be addressed. "Since you are not a hen and do have emotions and feelings, it is probably best if we get to know one another a little bit before we move on to the reproductive phase of our enterprise."

The woman laughed but nodded more enthusiastically than Hamilton appreciated.

"That would probably be best, thank you, sir."

Hamilton was left once again wanting to throw or hit something. It was an extreme reaction. He hadn't felt that confounded in years. Maybe not ever. He was stuck with the woman. He didn't want to find her attractive. But he did. He was torn between wanting her gone and wanting to start a family with her. He fervently hoped the passage of time would ease some of these frustrations because like it or not, he was stuck with her.

He was relieved that it was early fall. Hamilton would have plenty to keep him busy around the homestead while she got herself settled into his home. He could even leave. He had plenty of other business interests he could go check on. He needn't sit around watching her take over his home.

But he ought to keep an eye on her, or she might rob him blind.

The thought made him blink. Perhaps he was being slightly unfair. Just because she was so pretty it made his eyes ache didn't necessarily mean she was going to be a thieving liar. And besides, there wasn't much she could take. Being such a tiny little thing, he doubted she could carry off his furnishings, and those were easy enough to replace anyhow. He just wouldn't be giving her access to any of his bank accounts. That should keep him and his concerns safe.

He should have checked the westbound train schedule while they were at the station. She hadn't been here more than a couple of hours, and he was already itching to leave her behind. If only he hadn't made all the arrangements for his businesses in advance of her arrival for the very reason of not wanting to leave his new wife alone on the homestead. If he left now, it would be obvious to everyone that he was running away. Unless he got word from one of his businesses that there was a problem. But he couldn't fake that. He would jump at the chance to run away, but he had to man up and face this problem if no honorable way out was afforded him.

Chapter Three

"**S**o how come some of the men call you Hamilton and some call you Foster? Am I the confused one or are they?"

Her husband had been showing her around his homestead and introducing her to some of the workers. Sadie was becoming more and more confused. Some of them, like Herman, called him Foster. She just thought it was the male way of simplifying matters, dropping the Mister. But then some of the others called him Hamilton, which Sadie had understood was the man's first name. A name she had yet to use herself.

It was a shockingly ridiculous situation to find herself in. She was married to a man with whom she did not comfortable using his first name. It was a commentary on just how very desperate she had been. Which was why she had agreed so easily to her friend Jane Fredericksburg's suggestion that Sadie allow Jane's husband Fred to match her up with one of his friends. Sadie had been happy to agree to the protections afforded by the proxy marriage. In her mind, at the time, it seemed safer to be married prior to arriving into her new life in Nebraska. She had worried, if they weren't already married, the man might reject her, and then where would she be? When Fred had explained the legalities to her, that she would be a married woman as she travelled across the country, she had thought it sounded like a good idea. But now, here she stood, more than halfway across the country from anyone or anything familiar, married to someone that she wasn't even completely sure which name was his.

Ridiculous!

But there it was.

"My mother preferred the name Hamilton. It was her family name before she married my father. My father didn't object, although he did point out to her that giving me a name that's longer than our family name was sure to cause confusion. He wasn't wrong," he concluded with a low chuckle that caused a thrill of attraction to shiver down Sadie's spine. She ignored it.

"Do you have a preference? It seems others call you whatever they'd like."

"When I was a lad, my closest friends called me Ham or Milt. If you're asking what you should call me, I'll answer to any variation of either Hamilton or Foster, but I am partial to my first name, as fewer people use it." He paused for a moment. "I noticed you haven't really called me anything. Is that because you've been uncertain what to call me?"

Her laugh sounded nervous even to her own ears, but Sadie answered him. "Yes, you've been Mr. Foster in my mind, since the Fredericksburgs introduced us officially. But it sounded so formal that it made me uncomfortable."

"Well, despite our introduction, as you said, we really just met today, so I suppose it's understandable. Please, feel free to address me informally." He paused again before asking, "What would you like to be called? I suppose I ought to call you Mrs. Foster just to get used to the idea of having a wife."

The stricken expression on her face made Hamilton realize he had probably been a little too forthright. She needn't know he wasn't too sure about this marriage either. But then he was filled with relief when she giggled. It sounded a little hysterical, as though she were very nervous, but at least she didn't appear to be overly put out with him. He had no intention of ever giving her his heart, but if he were going to stay wed to the woman, it would be best if they could get along.

"Please, call me Sadie. I might not answer to Mrs. Foster at this point as I, too, am still adjusting."

They exchanged grins and Hamilton felt a flutter in the area he rather suspected might contain his heart. He ignored it. While he would try to give this woman the benefit of the doubt as Herman had suggested and not expect her to be as crooked as all the other pretty women he had ever known, he couldn't trust her nor love her.

Hamilton cleared his throat. "I forgot you were so hungry. We left something on the stove while we were gone so that you wouldn't feel obliged to begin cooking right away. We can finish your tour after you've had a chance to eat."

She again had that expression on her face that made Hamilton question what he had said, but he couldn't fathom what it might be. He was being polite and chivalrous, remembering to think of her needs over his own. She ought to be appreciative.

"Thank you, Hamilton," she finally replied in a prim tone of voice. "I would appreciate having something to eat. And while I do realize that I will have a role to fill here, which includes doing the cooking, I appreciate that you will allow me a little bit of time to adjust."

Hamilton felt his face relax into a grin. Now he understood why she had seemed a little put out. She didn't want to consider herself the labor force, he supposed. But what did she expect? No doubt, as such a pretty woman, she had expected to be waited on, rather than doing some honest labor. Well, she would have to realize that everyone needed to pull their own weight this far from the city. While he was a wealthy man, he didn't expect to have a pampered wife. It was one more reason he had asked Fred to provide him with a homely wife. He would have to send Fred a telegram as soon as possible. He needed to be sure he had gotten the right woman.

After she claimed to be filled up on what was to Hamilton's mind a very small amount of food, he showed her the rest of the nearby property. It was obvious she was tired, and he had no interest in taking her out on a trail and having her fall asleep in the saddle. If she even knew how to ride. Hamilton was afraid to ask. He had thought it was a good idea to marry someone from his hometown even though he had never met her. Now, he had to wonder where his mind had been. She hadn't even ever raised chickens before! And now she was going to be helping him run his homestead? It was a disaster waiting to happen.

He took a deep breath and tried not to panic. Nothing would be gained by overreacting. And really, the girl might not be as useless as she appeared. Fred must have had a reason for sending her, if she was, in fact, the one Fred had intended. Hamilton hadn't yet seen the paperwork for himself. But he could see that the woman was wilting before his eyes. He supposed it had been a long day for her. Hamilton would have to leave his lingering questions until the next day.

They had made a small meal of sandwiches from what was left of their earlier meal. Sadie had seemed sufficiently familiar with a kitchen, even if it might not be the top of the line type she was probably used to in the big city, that she had made herself useful by putting the small repast together for them. He had helped, of course. Despite being his legal wife, she was quite technically a guest in his house and ought to be treated accordingly.

But she was surprisingly good at making tea. And the sandwiches were perfect. She had spread the butter all the way to the edges of the bread, just how he liked it. But then she had nearly fallen asleep at the table. Hamilton only hoped she had managed to eat enough to make it through the night. He didn't think she had eaten more than half a sandwich. There already wasn't much to her. Hamilton sighed and escorted the woman up the stairs. He could feel her trembling as he held her elbow and he guessed at the cause.

"As we mentioned on the drive here from the train station and again with the animals, we are only just meeting. I don't expect either of us will feel comfortable being intimately acquainted until we're little better acquainted with one another. This will be your room for now." He indicated the open door they were standing in front of. She nearly sagged in her relief, reassuring Hamilton that he had hit on the source of her obvious anxiety.

"I'll see you in the morning. You're obviously beat. I have to check on a few things outside to make certain the men tightened everything up as they ought to."

She nodded and slipped into the room, shutting the door with nothing more than a whispered "Goodnight."

~ ~ ~

Sadie bustled about the kitchen, boiling water and wiping off the eggs she had enjoyed collecting a few minutes earlier. She rather thought she was going to enjoy that job. At least for as long as she was staying. Sadie sighed. Perhaps she ought to consider making it permanent. She felt her lips twist wryly. They were married. In all reality, that should be fairly permanent. No, she didn't really want a husband, and she had no intention of ever loving the man. But where else was she going to go? Sadie owed him a huge debt of gratitude for what he didn't even know he had done for her. She truly believed in loyalty and she owed that, at least, to him for the safety he was providing her. She shouldn't return his kindness by plotting a way to get out of the marriage.

Recalling his escort upstairs the night before, Sadie felt heat staining her cheeks that had nothing to do with the fire she had kindled in the stove. It was gracious of the man to offer her a space of time to get to know him before he expected her to perform certain marital duties. Of course, that might actually make it easier to get out of the marriage if she could figure out somewhere to go.

Sadie rejected the tempting thought. She would have to start thinking of reasons to stay rather than fantasizing about leaving. Hamilton seemed like a far more decent man than many of those she had encountered in Boston. He deserved her efforts to bring success to their union, not her attempts at escape.

Looking around the room she was in, Sadie felt her face stretching into what was probably a self-satisfied grin. She was lucky to be there. She needed to develop a sense of gratitude and respect toward Mr. Foster. Hamilton, she reminded herself. While it might sound a little odd to her ears, it wasn't uncommon for a man to have his mother's maiden name as his given name. In a certain way, it was rather nice. In this case, it was a bit of a mouthful, but she was certain she would grow accustomed to it. In fact, she decided then and there, it was a handsome name. With dignity. Just like the man himself.

She ought to learn more about him. All that Jane and her husband had told her was that an old friend of Mr. Fredericksburg was good friends with Hamilton. And that said old friend had spoken very highly of him. There was some sort of untold story involved, Sadie was certain of it. Jane had been adamant that Mr. Foster was a good man. He had done some sort of service to this old friend's wife. Another marriage that Mr.

Fredericksburg had arranged for another man with an interesting name. Ransom Delaney. Sadie found herself consumed with curiosity about the man, his name, and how Hamilton might have helped his wife. She wondered if Hamilton would tell her if she asked.

"That smells delicious."

Sadie nearly jumped out of her skin. She had been so deep in thought she hadn't heard him come down the stairs.

"Mr. Foster," she exclaimed, flushing deeply over his upraised eyebrow. "You startled me." She tried to explain before taking a deep breath. After expelling the pent-up air, she added in a steady voice, "Good morning, Hamilton, did you sleep well?"

She tried not to bristle over his obvious amusement with her discomfort. Sadie recognized laughter lurking in the depth of his gaze, but he kept a straight face.

"I didn't sleep the very best, but I'll feel much better after a cup of that coffee I can smell you are brewing."

Sadie hurried to prepare him a cup the way he had instructed her the day before while she clucked over him. "Oh dear, I'm sorry you didn't sleep that well. Do you often have trouble sleeping?"

"Not often," he answered briefly. "Must've had too much on my mind," he added, causing Sadie's color to deepen once again as guilt filled her. She was the problem, she thought, causing the poor man a sleepless night.

She offered him a weak smile. "I'm just about to cook up some eggs if you'll tell me how you like them."

"Have you already been out to collect them?" He seemed surprised, causing Sadie's flush to deepen.

"Is that all right? I didn't think it would matter what time I went, and I thought eggs for breakfast sounded delicious. But if you'd rather something else, I can probably fix you something, if you'll just tell me what you'd like."

Sadie was nervously chattering and couldn't seem to stop herself. She had thought she was being helpful by collecting the eggs already but perhaps he thought she was being disrespectful, not waiting for him to direct her. She hid her sigh of frustration behind a deep breath.

"Not at all, Sadie, I was just surprised. I would have expected you to sleep much later."

"Well, it was rather early when I retired. And I slept quite soundly. I haven't slept in such quiet in years, if maybe I ever did. It was quite lovely."

She couldn't interpret the strange expression on Hamilton's face, but Sadie ignored her own discomfort, smiled wanly at him, and proceeded to fry them both some eggs despite the fact that he hadn't told her what he wanted instead. She needed to eat soon despite the nervous tension in her stomach or she would get a headache.

Sadie didn't think she would be able to eat much, but was surprised by how delicious the small meal was. Her nerves pushed aside, Sadie made quick work of downing a couple eggs and a slice of bread.

"You did well."

Her face heating again, Sadie was embarrassed to hear how surprised he sounded.

"Did you not think I would? What did Mr. and Mrs. Fredericksburg tell you about me? Did they not tell you I could perform all the domestic necessities?"

He again had an expression she couldn't interpret. "They didn't say too much really, but yes, they did mention that my wife was highly skilled."

Sadie frowned, puzzled by his turn of phrase. When he didn't elaborate, she didn't press for more information, still embarrassed by his surprise. Her appetite was satisfied and her stomach was clenching from the familiar pang of nervous energy, so she got up and started tidying from the meal.

"Will you be all right here, Sadie? I have things I need to get done, but I don't want you to be nervous or uncomfortable."

"That's kind of you, but I'm sure I'll be just fine. I need to continue to familiarize myself with the kitchen, and it looks to me as though I will need to make some bread, so I'll have plenty to occupy myself with. Will you be around for a noon meal or should I pack you something to take with you?"

"Now you're the one being kind. I'm grateful that you're ready to get straight to work."

"Of course."

"I'll be back in a few hours." He finally answered one of her questions as he slapped his hat on his head and left the house.

~ ~ ~

Hamilton was grim as he strode toward the barn. He needed to wire Fred and confirm that this pretty, young woman was indeed his wife. He had to think of how to word the telegram. He should have asked her for the documents. He glanced back toward the house, thinking he ought to go in and do that before riding into the village. But he didn't want to get held up. She might get suspicious and have too many questions, and that would cause him delay. He would just have to come up with the proper wording on his own.

Normally he found the ride into the village to be restful. The scenery was lovely and he enjoyed the peace and quiet. But today it passed in a blur. Hamilton could hardly believe it when he found himself already in the village. He swung down off his horse, tied him to a post next to the watering trough, and walked directly to the telegraph office. It also happened to be the postal office and the mercantile, so pretty much the breeding ground for any and all gossip. Which was why he was wanting to be particularly careful about his wording.

PLEASE PROVIDE COMPLETE NAME OF EXPECTED ARRIVAL AND IDENTIFYING DETAILS. CAN YOU CONFIRM THAT MY INTENDED APPEARS AS REQUESTED?

It gave away more than he wanted, but that couldn't be helped. He wanted to reiterate that he wanted a homely woman but didn't want that getting around in the community. If the woman in his house really was his wife, he had no desire to shame her. Hamilton was rather proud of himself for how he had managed to word the telegram. No one would even know from his message that he had brought a woman home with him yet. While it was possible they had been seen while they drove through yesterday, the fact that they hadn't stopped would work in his favor now.

Hamilton hoped he wouldn't have to wait too long for a reply. It could be hours or days. But Hamilton didn't really want to go home without his answer. And he would hate for his reply to get intercepted by Sadie. If she was an imposter, he didn't want her to know he was onto her schemes. If she wasn't, it would surely hurt her feelings to find out what he had suspected. But Hamilton needed to know, so he nodded to the gentleman behind the counter and handed over the necessary coinage to pay for the message.

"I have some people and places to visit. I'll stop back in an hour to see if there has been a reply."

"Sure thing, Foster. I'll hold onto any messages for you until you tell me otherwise."

"Great, thanks." Foster flicked him another coin and walked out.

He glanced both ways along the dusty road when he stepped out of the store front. Hamilton was surprised by a giant yawn. He didn't really have anywhere pressing to go. Maybe he ought to just find a grassy spot under a tree somewhere and try to get a little bit more sleep before he came back and checked for a response from Boston. With a decisive nod, he untied his horse, swung up on his back, and rode out of the village to a small copse of trees. It would provide some shade and a bit of grass for the horse to nibble while he rested. Hamilton glanced at his timepiece trying to mentally prepare himself to wake up in the allotted time.

Releasing a groan from the discomfort of sleeping on the hard ground, Hamilton released another one when he realized it was a little more than an hour since he was at the mercantile. Not that it mattered overly much. The telegraph agent had promised to hold onto any messages until Hamilton returned. But Hamilton didn't want to risk someone else getting a message and, in an attempt to be helpful, riding out to his homestead right away. He hurried back hoping there was a message for him.

"Ah, Mr. Foster, you've got perfect timing," the man at the mercantile called to him when he stepped inside. "Come on back here. Your response has just arrived."

Hamilton glanced around, surprised to once again find the store free of customers.

"I've never seen it so empty in here, Smith."

"You never come in at ten o'clock in the morning." The other man chuckled. "It's usually crowded shoulder to shoulder when we first open at eight o'clock with anyone needing last minute provisions before they ride out for the day. And then again, it's fairly steady most of the afternoon. I've often thought we might as well just close from ten 'til one but then someone like you drops by, and I'm glad I didn't."

"Well, I'm glad you didn't as well. You said you'd already received the answer?"

"Just arrived not five minutes ago. A curious response. Not too many words. I trust you'll understand it better than I did."

Hamilton nodded grimly, glad the man wasn't exhibiting too much curiosity and relieved there were no women about. Not that there were many in the surrounding areas, thus his need to send to Boston for a wife, but there were wives around. Women that seemed to hunger for gossip. He wondered if it was a female issue or a result of being isolated. He gave a mental shrug. It didn't really matter why; he didn't want to be fodder for the gossips. Nor would he want his wife being discussed if he did have the proper woman at home.

"Thank you, Smith, I'm sure I'll figure it out."

SADIE AMELIA FITZSIMMONS

BLONDE AND BLUE

SILLY TINY HAT

BETTER THAN EXPECTED

Hamilton's stomach fell. Fred thought he was doing him a favor by sending him a pretty wife. He hadn't seen the papers that the woman no doubt had with her, but it seemed more than certain that the woman at his house was, in fact, his wife. For one thing, the silly, tiny hat was the sign Sadie had said she was to wear for him to identify her. Fred had originally just said she'd be wearing a hat. But the telegram proved that Fred had thought it a good joke at his expense. And the woman was definitely blonde and blue as the telegraph said. Her long blonde curls were probably outrageously fashionable in Boston, but they would be an encumbrance if she were going to do anything practical around the homestead. Her blue eyes were beautiful to behold. There was no avoiding that fact. Fred had sent him a beautiful woman as his bride. Once again, Hamilton felt a surge of violence welling up within him. He wanted to vent his frustrations with foul language or a wrestling match but had to content himself with deep breaths followed by a bruising gallop.

He slowed his mount and allowed the horse to cool down as they neared home. It wasn't the horse's fault Hamilton was in a predicament. When they reached the barn, Hamilton removed his saddle, wiped down his horse, and then let him loose into a field. He then set himself to the heavy task of replacing the straw in some of the stalls.

"What's going on, Boss?" Herman's voice interrupted the flow of his labor. Hamilton couldn't decide if he were relieved or disgusted. He took the time to wipe the perspiration that was streaming down his face with the back of his sleeve.

"What do you mean, Herman?"

"Well, for one thing, this should be Bobby's assignment, and for another, those stalls probably had at least another day or two in them before they needed to be replaced like that."

Hamilton wouldn't allow himself to feel any embarrassment or guilt over what he had done. He had enough money that even if he had to buy more straw, it wouldn't be a problem. And, as Herman had said, he was the boss, if he wanted the stalls cleaned out, and wanted to do it himself, it wasn't anyone else's place to gainsay him.

"Don't you have work to do?"

Rather than being chastised, Herman grinned at his boss, saluted him and left the barn without another word, adding to Hamilton's feelings of ill usage. By the time he got into the house, he was feeling overworked and cranky.

~~~

The slamming of the door made Sadie jump and nearly drop the pan she was holding. With a hand to her chest she turned to see what the ruckus was about.

"You startled me. Is everything all right?" Her newfound determination to make a go of her marriage prompted her to be solicitous. But it was a challenge in the face of the glower she encountered.

"Is there a reason you haven't given me the legal documents you were surely provided before boarding the train in Boston?"

Sadie felt the ready blush rising up once more into her pale cheeks. "No reason except that it slipped my mind with all the adjustments of a move like this." She paused, searching his face, wondering why he would be so mad about it. "I apologize if you were expecting me to hand them over immediately. They quite slipped my mind, in all reality." She began to untie her flour-splashed apron. "But I can get them for you right now." She suited her words to actions and hurried up the stairs while he stood where he was and watched.

For a brief moment, Sadie feared she had misplaced them. Wouldn't that be exactly what she needed, she thought with sarcasm. She knew they were important but was surprised at Hamilton's seeming anger. It wasn't as though she had deliberately withheld them. Her stomach clenched with nerves with the realization that she was married to such a volatile stranger. Despite her recent affirmation to herself that she would honor her vows, Sadie wondered if she would be able to remain with a man with an unpredictable temper.

As she dug through her bag, she was flooded with relief when her hand closed around the small bundle of papers. It was all the documentation Mr. Fredericksburg had assured her she would need. There was one bundle for her and one for Hamilton. Sadie wondered if she ought to give both to her husband but decided she might need her own copies for her own protection as her friend Jane, Mrs. Fredericksburg, had said when she insisted her husband provide two sets. Sadie remembered the encounter.

"Alastair Fredericksburg, you make another copy, right this minute," Jane had said with a sharp insistence. If Sadie hadn't heard the underlying warmth she would have thought her friend was upset with her husband.

"Now, Jane, you know Ransom vouches for this Foster fellow. There is nothing to be nervous about."

"I don't care who vouches for him. A woman can never be too protected. You know I'm right about this. And surely it won't take so very long to make one more copy. So, you needn't kick up a fuss."

Sadie had watched the byplay between the two and had been consumed with envy over the warmth between them. She wished she had a hope of such a happy union in her future but with how Hamilton was acting, Sadie knew she needed to keep her hopes low. She couldn't picture him ever looking at her with love in his eyes as Mr. Fredericksburg had looked at Jane.

With a nod and a sigh, Sadie gently buried her personal bundle of papers back at the bottom of her small luggage, under the scarf and mittens she had knitted on the train ride West in anticipation of the coming winter. She had dithered long enough. It was time to present the marriage documents to her husband.

"I'm sorry, Sadie, I shouldn't have growled at you like that." Sadie almost fell down the last few steps she was so surprised by Hamilton's words. "Despite the fact that I requested this arrangement, it seems to be a bigger adjustment than I had expected. But that's my problem, not yours, and I shouldn't be taking my frustrations out on you."

Sadie was at a loss as to how to respond to such unprecedented words. She could feel another blush staining her cheeks, so she avoided making direct eye contact with Hamilton, only bobbing her head in a small nod and quickly handing the bundle of papers over to him.

He scanned them quickly. "Your middle name is Amelia? I had an aunt named Amelia. It's a nice name."

How does one respond to such a statement? Sadie wondered. She smiled slightly and waited to see what else he would say, as tension gripped her. Her stomach clenched and her head began to ache as she watched him read through every line of words in the entire bundle of paperwork. He glanced up at her a couple of times while he was reading, making her wonder what he was thinking. Sadie almost sagged with relief when he finally lifted his head and put the bundle of papers down on the table.

"You look like you're about to faint," he commented with a frown. "Why is that?"

Sadie swallowed, wondering if she could avoid answering the question. But when he continued to gaze at her with elevated eyebrows, she was forced to stammer out a response.

"I don't really know you yet, but you appear to be upset. It is making me nervous."

"I already apologized for growling," he argued.

Sadie shrugged. "That doesn't change the fact that you seem upset. Are you wishing you could send me back to Boston?"

Her question was followed by silence, making Sadie want to hide. She had hoped he would laugh off her question as though it were ridiculous. But he stared at her instead. He finally spoke.

"Why would you ask me that? Are you wishing to return home? Are you sorry you came out to this backward countryside?"

"Don't put words in my mouth. It's you who is seeming to be upset about our marriage, not me. I only asked you a question."

"I need a wife. We're legally bound to one another, so no, I don't wish to send you back."

Sadie knew she should allow it to drop, but she just couldn't stop herself from asking, "Then why do you seem so upset?"

~~~

Hamilton stared at her in consternation. How was he supposed to answer such an unanswerable question? He cleared his throat, trying to hide his discomfort.

"As you said, it's a big adjustment taking a stranger to wife. And I must admit, you aren't what I was expecting."

He shouldn't have added that last bit. She appeared to suddenly be consumed with curiosity.

"What were you expecting? Did Mr. Fredericksburg lead you to expect someone with more accomplishments? I apologize if you feel you've been misled somehow."

Feeling heat climbing in his cheeks, Hamilton had no intention of admitting to her how very close she had come to the truth.

"Not at all, I didn't really have any sort of expectations."

The dubious expression on her face made Hamilton realize that he had just contradicted himself. He felt his cheeks burn but ignored the sensation. "What were you expecting from me when you arrived?" He hoped to turn the focus onto her.

She shrugged, her pretty face filling with embarrassment. "Mr. Fredericksburg didn't have a physical description of you, but he assured me you were a kind, successful, God-fearing man and that you would provide me with a place of security. That was all I could wish for."

Hamilton laughed. "I see Ransom was generous in his description."

Her confusion was evident, so Hamilton elaborated.

"My friend Ransom Delaney was the one who connected me with your friends the Fredericksburgs. He must have been generous in his description, if that's how I was described to you."

Now his wife was frowning. "Which of the descriptors was false?"

Hamilton would have gladly cut out his tongue but was forced to carry on. "Never mind about me, you're far prettier than I expected."

She appeared puzzled but flattered. Hamilton was relieved that women were always happy to hear such a thing. She was just like his mother had been. Hamilton suppressed the grimace of dismay that he felt forming on his face. It was his worst nightmare, so Hamilton forced himself to change the subject. Dwelling on the difficulties wasn't going to do either of them any good.

"It smells delicious in here."

She once again looked delighted. "Thank you. You were almost out of bread, so I baked some."

"You were able to find everything you needed?"

Her vigorous nodding would be endearing if he weren't so set against being drawn to her. "I am thrilled with how well stocked your larder is."

"Good, good," Hamilton answered, ready to be done with the frustrating conversation. What was he supposed to talk about with the tiny little woman? Why couldn't she have been the homely, desperate woman he had been hoping for? With a few more nods and murmurs Hamilton made good his escape, returning outside after grabbing a hastily scrambled together sandwich.

~ ~ ~

Sadie watched as her husband hurried out the door. She couldn't ignore the feeling that he was escaping from her. It was probably ridiculous, she tried to convince herself, but that was the impression she was left with as the door swung shut behind the man. He had barely even wanted to wait while she made him a sandwich. She had hurried to make it for him, not wanting him to go hungry even if he was strangely reluctant to spend any time in her presence.

She stood and gazed at the closed door as the latch clicked home. Once again, she was alone in the man's house. Sadie glanced around. It was a lovely house; she was indeed quite fortunate with where she had ended up.

As she had travelled West on the train her mind had been filled with images of all the possible outcomes of her rash decision to marry a stranger. None of her imaginings had come close to the reality. She had been afraid to be optimistic, even in her fantasies. But she couldn't feel she had been hard done by, that was for certain. If anything, Mr. Fredericksburg had been discrete in his explanation of Hamilton's circumstances. It was obvious this house and all that was in it was new. So unless the man had sold his soul to the bank or the devil, he was obviously doing well for himself, at least in the financial department.

As the train had travelled inexorably West, Sadie had watched the passing scenery. Many of the houses that could be seen from the train could barely even be called houses. Some had been shacks or hovels at best. It had filled her with both fear and determination. She was free of Oscar. She would make a better future for herself. And if that meant getting along with this stranger, then she could surely figure out how to do that. Her mother had always said that the way to a man's heart was through his stomach. Well, she could do that. It was one of the few things she was confident in for herself. She could cook. And in almost any circumstance. That was the one thing she had comforted herself with as she had seen those hovels. There had been smoke curling out of some of them, which meant there must be a stove of sorts. She had figured that had meant she wouldn't starve. But here she was, in the lap of luxury, really. No, it wasn't Boston, but then, what had Boston ever done for her except break her heart over and over again? No, she would make herself comfortable here in Nebraska. She knew it was a fine environment to form the foundation for her future.

Thus determined, she set to making her new husband the best supper he had ever had.

It wasn't even that hard in such a beautiful kitchen. Sadie was filled with gratitude that it wasn't hot out as she stoked the flames in the large stove. She would need to reconsider her cooking strategies by the time summer rolled around.

Chapter Four

Time flew by and before Sadie even realized it, she was feeling almost at home with Hamilton. Not actually with the man himself, of course, as he still seemed to be avoiding her, but Sadie had managed to meet the other women nearby and felt as though she were making friends. The forced isolation seemed to lead to immediate intimacy whenever she encountered another female. It would seem that the shared experience of being so far from civilization caused an immediate bond to form. Sadie couldn't tell if it was just women who experienced the phenomenon, but she found she quite enjoyed it. She felt immediately that the women she encountered were her friends and she could turn to them for help should she need it. It was a comfort to her, as she hadn't felt as though she had many friends back in Boston and she had no family anywhere, unless one counted her husband, of course, so the ready friendship with the few women she encountered was most welcome.

But those quick bonds also led to obligations. And Sadie always met her obligations. It was because of this that she found herself learning to harness the horses to the wagon. Herman was always willing to be of assistance to her, which kind of him, Sadie supposed, but she wasn't entirely comfortable with men, especially now that she was married. She was uncomfortable with her husband, of course, because he was a stranger, but she belonged to him now, so she tolerated his few appearances. Despite Herman's kindness, Sadie had no intention of cultivating a friendship with the man.

"You should have let me do that for you," he reprimanded from behind her.

"Thank you, Herman, but I wouldn't want to take you from your work. Besides, it's best if I know how to do things. I don't have any wish to burden anyone with my fidgets."

"You could never be considered a burden, Mrs. Foster. Besides, as the boss' wife, surely it could be considered part of my job description to help you."

Sadie couldn't help laughing over his words, but she ignored his attempts to replace her. "I can see your reasoning, Herman, but I still think it's best that I know how to do things. Besides, I'm nearly finished."

"I would be much more comfortable with checking to make sure it has been done correctly." He must have realized that he had just insulted her, as he turned an abashed face toward her. "No offence intended, ma'am."

"None taken. I do realize I'm a novice, so I suppose I should appreciate your checking it over."

"Serious injuries could happen either to you or the animals, ma'am," he continued to excuse.

Sadie stepped out of the way. "Please, check, I would appreciate it."

She hid her amusement over the pink tingeing the tips of his ears. The poor man was obviously still embarrassed.

"Could I pry into where you are going, ma'am?"

"Can I counteract your question with one of my own first? Why do you want to know?"

"If you run into trouble or don't return, I'd like to know where to start the search."

Sadie couldn't help laughing, despite the insult. "I appreciate your confidence in my abilities, Herman," she replied drily.

The pink from Herman's ears spread to his entire face.

"I do apologize, ma'am, I again mean no insult."

"And yet—" Sadie answered with another laugh. "But in answer to your question, I am taking some food items over to the Johnsons. I've heard Mrs. Johnson is very poorly, so I wanted to offer her a hand. I shouldn't be more than a few hours. Even if I stay to help her with some of her chores, I'll be home well before dark."

Herman lifted his hat in response to her words and then helped her into the wagon that he must have deemed was sufficiently harnessed to allow her to drive away.

Sadie did appreciate his concern. In some ways, it was nice to have someone worrying over her safety. But she didn't appreciate his assumption that she was incompetent. She didn't bother waving as she drove away.

~~~

"You aren't getting too attached to my wife, are you, Herman?"

"Not at all," Herman replied with a ready chuckle.

Hamilton knew his jealousy was irrational. It was one more reason why he shouldn't have gotten hitched to such a pretty woman.

"Might I ask, did Mrs. Foster say where she was headed?"

"I did ask her, although she didn't take too kindly to my question."

Hamilton laughed. "Why not?"

"She felt it implied a lack of confidence in her abilities as a driver."

Hamilton's laughter dried up, and he began to frown in confusion. "What does one have to do with the other?"

Now it was Herman's turn to laugh. "She wanted to know why I was asking, and I told her it was just in case something happened to her."

Hamilton nodded. "I guess I can see why she may not have appreciated that, but you weren't wrong. I'm glad you asked her. Did you get an answer from her?"

"I'm not sure if it was a complete answer, but she said she was taking food to the Johnsons. And she did have quite a basket of provisions with her, so it is likely she was saying the truth."

Hamilton was surprised and didn't hide it from his foreman.

"Do you find something objectionable about her going to aid Mrs. Johnson? Mrs. Foster mentioned she might be quite some time, as she aimed to help Mrs. Johnson with her chores, since she had heard the woman is in poor health."

"She never mentioned her intentions to me. That's rather foolish of her, isn't it? Who knows what sort of disease she'll bring home with her from there."

Herman shrugged. "She didn't seem to be concerned. The poor woman didn't seem to even think of the possibility. Do you think your wife is simple?"

Hamilton laughed shortly. "No woman is simple, Herman. Are you trying to ask if she's not quite right in the head?"

Herman shrugged again, obviously not wanting to admit to such a thought about his boss' wife.

"She might just be totally innocent and unaware of the risk she is running."

"Disease runs through Boston, doesn't it?"

"She may not have ever encountered it. I'll have to explain a few things to her when she gets home, that's for certain."

Herman nodded. "You could say it's mighty kind of her to be willing to help that poor family."

Hamilton nodded. Herman was right, he supposed, even if there was a chance she caught her death from the other woman. No one seemed to know what was ailing the poor woman, unless it was just her body giving out from producing child after child. While Hamilton would like to have a houseful of children himself one day, even he understood a woman needed a rest of birthing. Too many women died trying to bring another life into the world; it was obviously not easy on them. If that was what it was, then he needn't fear that Sadie would catch it, of course. But she should have asked him if he minded she go. Or at least told him of her intentions. Hamilton shook his head. He was probably being daft. He couldn't decide if he was worried for the woman or irritated with her.

After thinking about it all afternoon, Hamilton began to wonder if he should go collect his wife from the Johnson homestead. He couldn't settle to anything on his own property. And the drive home would afford him an opportunity to discuss with Sadie some of the dangers she was presenting to herself by traipsing about to all the sick within a couple hours' ride. This wasn't the first time she had done this. The only thing preventing him from doing so was how foolish she was likely to think him if he showed up there. But he was just about to throw his own pride to the four winds when he heard the wagon clatter into the yard.

He had been trying to keep himself occupied by examining all the tack and harnesses in the barn, so he was handy to her when she arrived. Hamilton stepped out of the barn and stared at her.

She looked exhausted. And well she should. It was nearly dark, he realized.

"Where have you been?"

He must have startled her because she nearly fell from the box of the wagon. Hamilton felt bad and hurried forward to help her down. She had one hand occupied with holding her basket.

"I'm sorry, Hamilton, were you expecting me sooner? I lost track of the time and then nearly got lost on the way home because my mind was drifting." He could feel her sigh rack her slight frame as he helped her down.

"No, no, I was just getting a little concerned about you as it was nearing dark. Are you all right?"

The smile she casted him rivaled the brilliance of the sun, and he almost had to wince.

"It was so great, Hamilton! The poor woman has so many children I nearly lost track of them all. But they are the sweetest little things and so appreciative of the little bit of attention I was able to give them. She's got another one on the way, probably any day now, so Mrs. Johnson just couldn't keep up with everything."

"So, you don't think she's truly ill?"

"It doesn't seem like it, just exhausted, poor thing. She slept most of the time I was there. The children helped me do all the chores, and then we did some lessons and played some games."

"You must be exhausted."

"I truly am," she said with such a happy grin that Hamilton frowned at her, puzzled.

"Why do you look so happy about it?"

"Well, for one thing, I'm likely to sleep like a hibernating bear tonight," she began with a laugh. "But for another, seeing someone else's misfortunes certainly puts your own into perspective, and then being able to help them with theirs is ultimately fulfilling, don't you think?"

Hamilton was still puzzled, but he nodded in response.

"What kind of misfortunes did you need put into perspective?"

Sadie's smile dimmed but she didn't run away from the conversation, which made Hamilton rather pleased.

"Any number of things, to be honest." She tried to pass it off lightly.

Hamilton realized he had grown tired of avoiding the young woman who was his wife and suddenly wanted to know more about her.

He tried to keep his tone gentle as he asked her, "Can you tell me about it?" He had thought she was a young, Society woman from the City, but her ready acceptance of life on the homestead and helping the neighbors was making him question his assumptions about her.

"Well, for one thing, I'm married to a man I barely know, but I don't live in a hut with six young children and barely any food to put on the table. With your comfortable situation here in this large house and all the chickens and cows, even if we do end up with many mouths, we'll be able to feed them without difficulty."

"I swear to you, I will make sure you don't end up in the same situation as Mrs. Johnson."

Her sunny smile returned. "I know," she answered simply.

"Mrs. Johnson was also a mail order bride, but she didn't have the luck I did. She was even more alone than I was, so she didn't have anyone to vouch for her husband. She merely answered an advertisement in the paper. I, at least, had the Fredericksburgs to advise me and recommend you."

"They were all you had to advise you?" Hamilton was appalled when she nodded and shrugged.

"Everyone else has died."

"I had no idea."

He couldn't believe it when Sadie chuckled. "I hope you weren't expecting a visit from any in-laws, as I am all you got."

"Who did you lose?"

"The simple answer would be to say everyone. But, that's an oversimplification, as there are relatives in Ireland who would probably be happy to claim me, but no one on this side of the ocean. My parents came here as newlyweds. My brother arrived not long after they did. From what I understand, he was a sickly baby and he never got strong. Then they had me. My mother always said I was too stubborn to ever catch anything. We lost my brother when I was five. Mama never really recovered from that loss even though she had me and my sister. When I was twelve, my father died in an accident. Mama tried to work for a few years, but we struggled for food and shelter, so I can really empathize with Mrs. Johnson's predicament. For the past five years I've been working as a seamstress and nursing my mother. But then my sister caught the flu and brought it home to Mama. They both died this year. But the doctor's bills were more than I could handle, so I found myself in a bit of a pickle."

Hamilton wanted to laugh over her turn of phrase, but there was nothing in the least bit funny about the story she had just told. If she was telling the truth, there was nothing about her that he had expected from her appearance. She was clearly not afraid of hard work. He had already seen that with his own eyes, even before she had spent the day slaving for the worthless Johnsons.

"Do you plan to return to the Johnsons?"

He didn't care for the hesitant way Sadie looked at him. But then she rushed into speech. "I would like to, if you wouldn't mind terribly. I know I should have asked you, especially since I gave away some of your own provisions and I have no way of paying you for them, but I had the impression that you believed in being neighborly and wouldn't mind."

"I don't mind the little expense. I just would have preferred if you had mentioned your plans to me. I didn't really appreciate hearing about it from Herman."

Sadie hung her head. "I'm sorry, that wasn't well done of me, was it?"

"Nope," he said. "Why did you feel you needed to hide it from me?"

Sadie chewed her lip and seemed to contemplate her answer. Hamilton tried to ignore how attractive she looked, as he was almost certain she was about to lie to his face.

"When I heard about their poverty and problems from one of the other neighbors, I think I associated them with myself and my own history. There is a sense of shame with being that poor. No one wants to take handouts from others. I was never really offered any charity, but I hated not being in a position to help others, not even my neighbors. It's shameful. But being able to help Mrs. Johnson today filled me with pride that I'm not in that situation anymore. I couldn't have borne it if you had denied me. So, I didn't ask." She lifted her head, and Hamilton could read a storm of emotions waging behind her eyes. "I'm not sorry I went to help her, but I'm sorry that I did it behind your back. And really, I guess my pride was misplaced since it was your largesse that I was taking to her, not my own, and you didn't even give me leave to do so."

Hamilton couldn't bear to see her happiness dimming. Without thinking about it, he reached out and clasped the hands that she had begun wringing.

"Don't feel badly about it, Sadie. We're married now. Mine is yours. You don't have to ask my permission to share what we have with others. You were absolutely correct when you assumed that I believe in sharing with my neighbors. We have been blessed with much. This brings an obligation not to hoard it. But I only ask that you let me know where you're going to be. It's a matter of safety. And really a matter of convenience," he added with a chuckle. "I won't be able to accomplish much if I have to worry about your whereabouts." He was relieved that rather than taking offence she laughed along with him.

"I promise to tell you the next time."

"Maybe I'll come with you next time, then."

"Really?"

Hamilton was surprised to see how eager she appeared. "Why do you look so surprised?"

"I didn't think you had much regard for Mr. Johnson."

"I don't. He's a useless waste, in my opinion, but those six, soon to be seven, small children didn't ask for their circumstances. And winter is coming. They won't survive if we don't help them."

Sadie still appeared hesitant. Hamilton tried to be patient as he waited to see if she would express her thoughts.

"Could we maybe go next week?"

"Sure, we can. We're not so very busy around here right now. And we have enough men to do whatever is necessary anyway." He surprised himself when he added, "If you don't want to wait a week, we could go sooner, if you want."

"Really?" she asked again, setting Hamilton's teeth on edge. He might not trust her, but he wanted her to trust him. Perhaps he was being a hypocrite.

"Really. You name the time, and I'll go with you."

The grin she gave him was all the payment he needed. Which angered Hamilton. He shouldn't be so easily swayed by a pretty smile.

"Maybe in a few days," she answered eagerly. "I don't want to allow my chores around here to slip, and also I'd like to prepare some supplies for them, so that will take some time."

"Today's Tuesday. Will you be ready by Friday?"

Her vigorous nodding made him smile. His smile stretched into a grin when she suddenly yawned, and it seemed to surprise her.

"You're going to fall over if you don't get yourself off to bed soon. Maybe I shouldn't let you go over there if it's going to exhaust you."

"I'll be fine," she assured him earnestly. "I'll be better prepared next time. Besides, I'll have you with me."

He was humbled by her trust.

"Are you going to be able to eat some supper or are you going straight to bed?"

Suddenly she appeared affronted.

"I'll not be shirking my responsibilities just because I enjoy helping the other women in the area. I didn't mean to be gone quite so long, but I did prepare for our supper before I left. I can have it on the table in fifteen minutes. I just have to clean up first."

"If you tell me what you had planned, I can get things started while you're doing that."

Her surprise turned to shyness. "That's not necessary, at all, Hamilton. I can surely manage."

"I suppose we are a team. It's fine."

She seemed to like his words, offering him another shy smile.

"You could put the kettle on and make sure the fire is stoked, and I'll be right down." With those words, she hurried into the house before he could say anything more. With a shake of his head, Hamilton followed her into the house at a slower pace.

Chapter Five

"There's something you need to hear about, Boss."

"What is it, Herman?"

"There is a man in the village asking about Mrs. Foster."

Hamilton stopped what he was doing and turned to glare at his foreman. "What do you mean there's a man asking about Sadie? What kind of man? What is he asking?"

Herman held up his hand. "I don't really know. The postman told me when I was there. I figured you would want to know."

Hamilton frowned, looking around. "She's not here or we could ask her about it."

"She might not know anything about it. How would she know who might be asking about her?"

"Nobody ought to be asking about my wife."

"You're not sounding completely rational now, Foster. Maybe I shouldn't have told you."

"Of course, you should have. Never mind, we'll get to the bottom of it."

~ ~ ~

Sadie was just about to climb into the wagon when a voice behind her made the blood chill in her veins.

"Life in the West seems to agree with you Miss Fitzsimmons."

She turned slowly to face the man, wishing for the first time in her life that she had a gun in her hands. Fear filled her, but she tried to remain rational as she battled to stay calm.

"Hello, Patrick. I never expected to see you so far from Boston."

"Oscar sends his regards."

"I have no wish to receive his regards, thank you all the same."

"Still so uppity, despite everything, I see."

Fear almost choked her as the man stepped closer to her, but Sadie fought to hide it. "I really must be going."

"What do you think your new husband would think if he heard about the rumors that swirled around you in Boston?"

"Those rumors were untrue slanders, probably made up by you or Oscar."

The man shrugged. "Many people believed them."

"No, they didn't," she protested weakly. "There was no one who would care what was said about me one way or the other."

"Your husband would care."

Sadie tried to keep her voice cold and steady as asked, "What do you want, Patrick?"

"I'm trying to fund my trip further West to see if there's any more gold to be found. I think you ought to help me out."

"Why would I do that? And what makes you think I have access to anything that might help you anyway?"

"I've heard enough about your husband to know you have access to plenty. And I'm quite sure you wouldn't want him having any doubts about you."

Sadie didn't say anything in response, merely turning her back on the bounder and climbing into the wagon, as she should have done right from the start.

"I'll be in touch," he called after her, chuckling as she slapped the reins on the horses back, prodding them into a faster pace. She had no desire to hurt the poor beasts, but she needed to get as far away from the reminder of her past as quickly as she could possibly manage. She felt the urge to have a bath to wash the experience off herself, but she had to force herself to a calm she didn't feel.

Sadie's mind was exploding in panic. She and Hamilton had been making so much progress in getting to know one another. Despite her original resistance to remaining in the marriage, every day she had more reasons to be glad she had done so. And even though she never wanted to love another after the pain of the losses she had experienced, Sadie felt drawn to the strong, handsome man who was her husband.

But she knew he resisted warm feelings toward her. Every time they seemed to be drawing closer together, it was as though he caught himself and tried to pull further back, colder toward her for a day or two until he relaxed his guard and they had a warm moment again.

If Hamilton were to meet Patrick, he'd never warm up to her again.

Sadie was fairly certain Hamilton was trying not to like her. She couldn't put her finger on why she thought that, as it seemed rather ridiculous. The man sent for her. It wasn't her idea. She hadn't imposed herself upon him in anyway. One would think he would want to like his wife. One could even be excused for thinking he might want to love her. But it seemed every time they shared a good experience or seemed to be enjoying spending time together, he clammed up and avoided her for a day or two. It was disconcerting to say the least.

Sadie would think he wasn't quite right in the head if not for the fact that she had reason to believe he was hugely successful as a businessman. She was making assumptions, of course, as he was never willing to discuss his business or finances. Not that she wanted to pry into his affairs, but as he had said his house was her house, she rather thought that might apply to everything he owned. But it didn't really matter. She didn't need anything as long as she was fed, clothed, and housed. It wasn't as though she would understand his business affairs if he were to tell her about them anyway. Of course, he could explain them, she thought with a little huff.

Not that these thoughts were at all conducive to her purpose. Sadie gave her head a shake as she slowed the wagon to nearly a walking pace. She needed to think before she got home. What was she going to do about Patrick? How had he found her? And why? What could possibly make him think she could give him any money?

What was she going to tell Hamilton?

This was the only question that mattered. If she thought there was a way she could get away with not telling him, she absolutely would avoid it at nearly any cost.

She still hadn't come to a clear decision by the time she saw the house in the distance.

~~~

Hamilton watched his wife drive the carriage into the yard. It was obvious she had been crying.

"What has happened?"

The tears, which had dried before she arrived, began to fall again much to Hamilton's dismay. He had already nearly reached the wagon but when he saw her face crumple, he closed the distance with long strides, reaching for her and pulling her from the wagon. Barely checking his pace, he hurried toward the house.

"What has happened? Are you hurt?" He ignored how good it felt to have her in his arms. She even seemed to snuggle in, as though she wanted to burrow into him, as though she too was enjoying the contact. But Hamilton couldn't become distracted by the pleasure, as she was clearly upset. He tried to pull back to look into her face. "Where are you hurt?"

"In my heart," she finally said through her tears, and Hamilton nearly dropped her. Now they were decidedly out of his depth. He wished he hadn't seen her arrive in this state. He had no idea how to cope with it.

He still had her in his arms when he sat down on the stairs of the porch. He didn't really want anyone to witness the scene that was about to unfold, but he couldn't really manage carrying the weeping woman and opening the door. Now that he was thinking about it, it was probably possible, but his brain could barely manage the task of not throwing her as far as possible, which was his first instinct. He would rather wrestle an angry bear than try to comfort a crying woman. But he was stuck with one now. He would have to muddle through.

Clearing his throat, Hamilton tried to think of something to say.

"Do you want to tell me about it?"

"No," was her less than helpful response.

"Why not?" While he didn't want to be in this situation, he didn't like the thought of her keeping things from him.

"Because you're not going to like it." Her answer prompted even more weeping, much to Hamilton's dismay.

"Well, I don't like your crying, so it's not likely to get worse."

Hamilton wanted to snatch back the words as soon as they left his mouth but to his surprise, they seemed to stem her tears. She actually laughed a little, even if it was a little watery. But at least her sobs had subsided.

She pulled back to look him in the face. He pulled out what he hoped was a clean handkerchief from his pocket and tried to wipe her face. She looked so very woe begotten that Hamilton's heart actually clenched in his chest.

"It can't be as bad as all that. Come now, tell me and we'll find a solution."

Tears continued to leak from the edges of her eyes but she didn't make any more sobs as she examined his gaze seriously, as though to gauge the sincerity of his words. She finally nodded.

"I don't want to keep secrets from you. You are my husband, after all. But this is just so dreadful that I would keep it if I could."

"You're right, you shouldn't keep secrets," he promptly replied, ignoring the prickling of his conscience over all that he was keeping from her.

She sighed and took a deep, shuddering breath before speaking. "I don't know if he came after me specifically or if he has just decided to stop in because it was convenient, but there's a terrible man from Boston here in the village, and I'm fairly certain he intends to blackmail me."

Hamilton blinked. Even though Herman had warned him someone was asking about Sadie, he hadn't expected her to tell him about it, at least not like this. He cleared his throat again, uncomfortable with the need to offer her comfort.

"Why does this hurt your heart? Did he threaten you in some way? Or did you have feelings for this man in the past?" He tried not to sound angry, but a wave of jealousy rose up within him and it was difficult to suppress. His own feelings almost made him miss the shiver of obvious revulsion that passed through her.

"The only feelings I have for him are angry ones. I've tried really hard not to hate him, but it's difficult."

Hamilton was no closer to feeling enlightened. "What makes you think he will try to blackmail you?"

"Because he did."

Hamilton's arms flexed around her. "Someone accosted you in the village?"

He could see her features filling with worry over his obvious anger, but he couldn't help it. No one had any right to frighten his wife. Not even him, he tried to remind himself in an effort to restrain his fury.

"Did he lay his hands on you?"

She shook her head vigorously. Hamilton took a deep breath and tried to keep his voice low and steady.

"Maybe you ought to just tell me everything from the beginning."

She again stared into his eyes as though trying to read his soul. "What will you do when you get mad?"

"I'm not going to get mad."

"You will, so I want to know what you'll do."

"I might get mad just from this question," he replied.

She actually giggled. Hamilton's heart clenched again. She was the sunniest person he had ever encountered. He squeezed her once more.

"Listen, sweetheart—" They both blinked over his use of the endearment, but he ignored it and continued, "I promise, if you tell me the truth, I won't get mad about what you say. Well, I won't get mad at you, all right? But you have to tell me everything, every single detail, do you understand? I might get mad about the situation, or at this man, but I promise I won't be angry with you."

"How can you be sure?" she whispered, more tears swimming in her eyes but this time she managed to keep them from falling.

"Because I'm beginning to see that you aren't the sort that would cause someone to be angry." He couldn't go into the details with her now, but he was starting to suspect she might be a special woman, nothing like his mother, despite the fact that there was a strange man in the village asking about her, probably the same one who was trying to blackmail her.

Her pretty forehead continued to be marred by a worried frown but she nodded, took a deep breath, and tried to explain.

"Remember, I told you about my mother and sister and the doctor's bills?"

Hamilton nodded but didn't interrupt, hoping she could tell him the problem, realizing suddenly that this was stemming from Boston and rooted in an emotional mire he would much rather not tread through.

Her voice wavered, but she continued. "We had to move to a worse part of the city when they got sick because we could barely afford the rent. As it was, I was always behind on something. If I bought food, I couldn't pay the rent. If I paid the rent, I couldn't pay the doctor. The doctor was so kind and was willing to take small payments each week, but I still could never get caught up. Our landlord wasn't kind. He kept making me offers." She hesitated and could no longer look at him as one of the tears finally escaped and trickled down her salty cheeks. She took another shuddering breath. "Unacceptable offers. It would have solved our problems, but I just couldn't do it. The only thing I had left was my honor. I don't know if I did the right thing. Maybe if I had been able to get them better or more food they would have survived. Or if I could have bought more medicine. But I just couldn't do it."

Hamilton's throat hurt as he forced the words out, trying to be gentle. "You absolutely did the right thing. Surely you realize your mother and sister would never have wanted you to..." He couldn't even say it. "And if the doctor was so kind, he surely would have ensured you had enough medicine for them."

"I don't know, Hamilton. Oscar finally tried to put more pressure on me by starting rumors that I had already done what he was asking of me. So, he said I might as well since already everyone believed it. And people did believe it, Hamilton." She looked at him with heartbreak in her eyes, and Hamilton wanted to weep at the sight. "The doctor didn't come around as often, and then I was fired from my job."

It was all Hamilton could do not to bellow with rage over her ill treatment, but he tried to remain calm so she would tell him the rest.

"I'm certain that was Oscar's intentions. If I was truly desperate, he probably thought I would finally have to do what he said. But by then Mama and Sister were dead. So there was nothing left to fight for. And then Jane said I could marry you, and I was able to pay off all the bills and come here."

He tried to keep the anger out of his voice but he had to ask, "Did you pay the rent, too?"

"I am a woman of honor," was all she said, but he could hear a note of pride in her voice despite all the sorrow.

He realized she truly was. Her honor wouldn't allow her to run away without paying all of her bills. But that was why his bride had arrived with so few possessions and an empty stomach despite the money he had sent.

Chapter Six

Hamilton fidgeted. He had been avoiding Sadie for a week. Really, one could say he had been avoiding her since she had arrived. He knew she had noticed, but he couldn't help himself. Of course, he went in and ate whatever meals she had prepared whenever she rang for him. But with as few words as he could get away with, he gulped down the food and then was back out the door.

The meals were delicious. Far better than he ever could have prepared. But Hamilton could barely stand her watchful gaze as she stared at him, clearly aware that he was trying to stay far away from her.

She had been in Nebraska, in his home, for more than a month. Five weeks, if one was counting. Hamilton felt like there weren't enough chores in the world to get him through the day and away from Sadie. He was trying to resist the pull she had on him but was failing rather miserably. He was just about to pack up and head out to California to check on his mining operations as an excuse to create the needed space. Surely there was something requiring his attention there even if he hadn't yet received word.

"Running a homestead takes a great deal of work, doesn't it?" Her soft voice stalled him from getting up from the table.

He glanced at her, wondering where she was going with this question as he felt guilt niggling at his conscience.

"Nothing that we can't handle."

"I feel badly that I'm not helping more."

Hamilton frowned at her. "What do you mean?"

Sadie shrugged. "I'm not doing very much."

"Seems to me you're doing plenty. You keep our clothes clean and mended. The house is always filled with delicious smells from whatever you're cooking. You look after the hens and chicks very well."

She shrugged again. "It still doesn't seem to be enough. I have plenty of time to gad about visiting the neighbors and still get all that done."

"I wouldn't exactly call it gadding about when you're taking food and help to the neighbors."

"But couldn't I be helping you more? I feel like you're going to work yourself to death. I can hardly believe how much work you do. Surely there are some tasks I could look after for you so you don't have to be working so much."

Now Hamilton's guilt nearly swamped him. He didn't want his wife working too hard, either. And he was making up work for himself just to avoid her. Herman was forever laughing at him for it.

"With winter coming, there will be plenty of time to be sitting around," he told her with a sinking sensation. He couldn't leave her here to fend for herself, but he dearly wished he could be in California for the winter this year.

"Are the winters particularly harsh around here? I've been trying to prepare with making preserves and things, but I'm not sure if I'm doing enough."

"You're doing plenty, I'm sure, and we'll be able to get out to the mercantile even during the winter. While we will get plenty of snow, and you wouldn't want to get caught too far from home when a storm comes up, the winters aren't so very harsh."

Watching her chew her lip with indecision nearly tore Hamilton apart inside. He hated the fact that he was making her insecure. Or should he say, even more insecure. It had been obvious from the stories she had told him about her life in Boston that she had some emotional baggage. And his attempts to avoid her were not helping with that. Now it was Hamilton's turn to fidget.

"Would you like to meet my friends? The ones who vouched for me with the Fredericksburgs?"

"The Delaneys?" she asked, surprising Hamilton with her knowledge. At his nod she responded eagerly. "I would love to. Are they coming to visit?"

"I was thinking we could go visit them." He didn't regret it when she appeared delighted by the idea, even though she appeared a little hesitant, too. It was obvious that although she was nervous, she also wanted to meet his friends. Or maybe she just wanted to meet other people. Either way, he probably should have made her feel more comfortable before now.

"Thank you, I would like that very much. When would you like to go?"

Hamilton shrugged. "I can't decide if I want to surprise them or send a telegram. What do you think?"

She looked at him rather dubiously for a moment. Hamilton couldn't blame her. He had been avoiding her quite obviously for weeks, and now he was inviting her on a trip and asking her opinion. Sadie's tinkle of laughter filled him with relief. He hadn't heard it in what seemed ages, and it was such a beautiful sound.

"Not knowing your friends, I can't really answer that question. Are they the type that would appreciate a surprise?"

"I think so. They did tell me I'm always welcome in their home. And I know Hannah would appreciate some adult female association."

"I take it she has young female association?"

Hamilton laughed. "Yes. Her young sister and Ransom's niece. And their new baby is a girl, too. But she is always happy for company." He paused for a moment, feeling uncomfortable. "I think you'll like them."

~ ~ ~

Sadie watched Hamilton's face attentively. He often hid his thoughts, but this evening it was obvious to her that he was wondering how it happened that he spoke his thoughts aloud. He had been so busy lately that she had barely spent any amount of time with him. She rather suspected he had been keeping himself diverted so he wouldn't have to be around her.

She couldn't blame him. With her background, he probably regretted their commitment. He was no doubt ashamed to have a wife who was being blackmailed. That was why his invitation to meet his friends had been such a surprise. She would love to meet the Delaneys. The Fredericksburgs had spoken so highly of them. Sadie knew Mr. Fredericksburg had arranged their marriage, just as he had done for her and Hamilton. She rather thought it strange that a man was matchmaking for his friends, but it was sweet in a certain way. In either case, she was looking forward to it, if Hamilton actually followed through and took her.

He cleared his throat, making her jump a little as she had gotten caught up in her own thoughts.

"How soon do you think you could be ready for a few days away?"

Sadie waved her hand in dismissal. "In a few minutes, I would imagine."

Hamilton laughed. "I suppose so, considering you didn't bring much with you. I guess this is one reason to be grateful for that."

Feeling heat fill her face, Sadie avoided his gaze, waiting to hear what he had decided.

"Very well, let's surprise them, then. We'll leave at first light the day after tomorrow. I'd like to spend the day tomorrow making arrangements with the men here to make sure the winter preparations carry on without us."

Sadie nodded, turning back to the kitchen to clear up from the supper. She had gotten used to Hamilton leaving immediately after rushing to gobble up whatever she had cooked. This was the longest he had lingered since her first meal in the house.

She heard him clearing his throat again, something she noticed he did whenever he was uncomfortable.

"Thank you for the supper. It was delicious, as usual."

Sadie appreciated his politeness. Even when he was rushing to get away from her, he always took a second to express his thanks.

"You're welcome, Hamilton. Thank you for talking with me a little."

She was surprised to see pink tinge his ears at her words. He quickly jammed his hat on his head and strode from the house. Sadie sighed as she watched him leave. She was getting mightily bored on her own. She felt obliged to make as many preparations as possible for the coming winter, thus confining her visits to other homesteads and neighbors to once per week.

It had been wonderful when Hamilton had accompanied her once. The second time she had visited the Johnsons he had gone with her as he had promised. It had been obvious to her even then that he was uncomfortable around her, and it had only worsened after that trip. Sadie had no idea what she had done to give him a disgust of her. She had thoroughly enjoyed the day. It had felt as though they were working toward a common goal. Neither of them had any preconceived notions, although Sadie had already been to the Johnsons' property. So, it turned out, had Hamilton.

It felt to her they were working harmoniously as he performed the more rigorous chores around the property, making some repairs and rearranging some furniture within the house to make room for the growing family. At the same time, Sadie had cleaned and done the laundry while also teaching the children some math and reading them a story. Then Hamilton had joined them for a meal, and then they had played with the children for a while before leaving.

Sadie had enjoyed the day quite thoroughly. Watching Hamilton with the children had been a delight. She appreciated how he listened to them attentively, even the smallest child who could barely talk yet. It had been cute to see his brow furrowing as he tried to understand the little tyke and respond appropriately.

But then, when they'd climbed into the wagon to return home, he had barely said a word. Sadie had thought he was maybe worn out, so she hadn't badgered him with chatter. But then his silence had continued. It wasn't as though he had been overly chatty before then, but Sadie noticed a difference. They had been speaking little by little each day, getting to know one another. But after their trip to the Johnsons', Hamilton exchanged only the fewest words possible with her.

It was disconcerting. Sadie had no idea what she had done to displease him, if anything. Perhaps he had just absorbed what she had told him about Oscar, and he no longer considered her a worthy partner. Or he hadn't liked how she had behaved with the Johnson children. But when she had tried to ask him about it he had brushed off her concerns saying there was nothing wrong. Sadie thought back to that awkward but brief conversation.

"Are you still thinking about what I told you about Oscar and Patrick?"

"No, and I don't want you to ever speak their names again. They are not worthy of your thoughts."

Sadie had nearly fallen out of the wagon with her surprise over his conflicting sentiments. Only Hamilton's quick, warm clasp of her arm saved her from certain injury.

"You aren't to give them another thought, Sadie, promise me. The matter is no longer of your concern."

She had blinked and nodded, feeling warmed and chilled at once. Sadie rather thought if the man would talk to her just a little bit more she would be in danger of falling in love with him. While he regularly hurt her feelings with his apparent lack of interest, when he did pay some attention to her, it warmed her heart and filled her head with nonsensical ideas. The fact that he wanted her to promise not to even think of the two heinous men was charming. But the cold, hard tone of his voice when he said it was not her concern distanced her. She nodded her agreement but sighed quietly, wondering how he expected her to keep such a promise.

Sadie blew the lock of hair off her forehead that had escaped her braids. Agonizing over it wasn't going to do her any good. He had invited her to accompany him to meet his friends. She would have to regard that as a promising change. And they would be confined together for the time of the travel. She had no way of knowing how far away the Delaneys lived, but since he said they'd be gone for a few days, it was obviously more than an hour or two away. Butterflies fluttered to life in Sadie's midsection as she anticipated the travel time. It could be wonderful if he chose to talk with her or incredibly awkward if he didn't. Shrugging away the unhelpful thoughts, Sadie set to work finishing the chores that needed to be done before she could retire for the night.

Chapter Seven

"**I**'m sorry you've arrived when we're all at sixes and sevens."

"No, it is we who should be apologizing." Sadie was struggling to hold onto her composure. It had been a long drive. Hamilton hadn't had much to say, offering the fewest words in answer to any of her attempts at conversation. And their surprise to his friends had fallen a little flat. Hannah's sister was sick and the household was in disarray. "Arriving unannounced as we have, we cannot expect you to be prepared for us."

Sadie was nearly beside herself with discomfort. She hadn't been able to prevent herself from asking Hamilton about Patrick during their journey. She had sat through the first couple of hours of the drive, barely tolerating the awkward silence that had been broken only by her stilted questions followed by Hamilton's barely grunted responses. Finally, when she could no longer help herself she had blurted out her question.

"Are you going to hate me forever because of my past?"

"What are you talking about?" It was the longest sentence he had spoken to her all day. "I could never hate you."

"You act like you do. You must be disgusted with me because of Patrick. No upstanding woman would have a blackmailer."

The sound that followed her statement sounded almost like a growl. "I thought I told you not to even think about him."

Sadie snorted. "That's easier said than done. You haven't spoken to me since I told you."

She couldn't quite interpret the expression on his face as he gazed at her. He looked stricken by her words, and his pink cheeks reflected embarrassment. Before she could wonder further he cleared his throat loudly.

"You needn't worry about Patrick ever accosting you again. I told him your debts were paid and no one in these parts would ever believe there was ever anything impure about you, not that they would care if there had been. I then thrashed him for coming near you and sent him on his way."

"Oh no, Hamilton, I'm so sorry."

"What on earth are you sorry for?"

"I've caused you so much trouble. I had no idea you had gotten into an altercation with him."

She watched as he flexed his fingers on the reins and turned to her with a grin. "It brought me the greatest pleasure, I can assure you."

Sadie opened her mouth to protest but shut it quickly when Hamilton interjected. "Now, put it from your mind. I don't want you thinking about another man."

She was stumbling out a disjointed protest that no other man was on her mind but him when he interrupted her rambling thoughts with his statement. "We're nearly there, I'm fairly certain the smoke curling from behind those trees is probably from Ransom's chimney."

Sadie squeaked and started patting her head, hoping she wasn't a windblown disaster after three hours in the wide open air on the wagon.

With a blink, Sadie brought her attention back to what their hostess was saying.

"I'm thrilled to have you here, though, please don't mistake me. And I know Ransom will be as well, once he gets here."

Sadie could see her hostess' eyes flitting around at the few scattered items that were clearly out of place while her hands fluttered around her head, trying to capture the strands that had escaped.

"Would you mind having a seat while I tidy up a bit and put the kettle on?"

Sadie wished they could just offer to return home, but that would probably be insulting to Hamilton's friends, besides the thought of three more hours bouncing around in the wagon made her feel slightly ill. Racking her mind to think of the best solution, she tried to smile warmly at the other woman.

"Why doesn't Hamilton show me around to your small animals, and we come back in an hour or so? Then you'll have a little more warning that you're about to have guests, and we'll have stretched our limbs after the long drive."

Hannah's face crumpled in an expression of regret and relief. Sadie interrupted the further apologies that were obviously on the way.

"And we would love a cup of tea or coffee when we return, thank you so much for offering."

Without allowing the other woman to say anything more, Sadie grabbed Hamilton's elbow and practically dragged him from the house. She could feel his incredulous gaze upon her but didn't stop walking until they were well away from the house.

"That was interesting," Hamilton finally said in a mild tone.

"We obviously should have sent that telegram," Sadie countered.

Hamilton shrugged. "You're being too sensitive. She was happy to see us and so will Ransom be when he gets in from the fields."

"She was obviously happy to see you, but I think she was a little thrown off to see you had a wife in tow."

Hamilton was looking at her quizzically, and Sadie felt heat flooding her face. "Are you feeling awkward or jealous, Sadie? That would be unwarranted on either count, I can assure you."

"Well, I'm certainly feeling awkward about arriving unannounced to a household with a sick child. For one thing, I'm sure it's uncomfortable for the hostess, no matter how happy she might be to see you. For another, there's a very good chance we'll catch whatever illness is going through them and either have a miserable drive home or be stuck here with them, adding to their discomfort."

Hamilton just laughed. "You are a worrier. I have the constitution of an ox."

Sadie raised her eyebrows. "And maybe the thick skull of one, too," she muttered, uncertain how to respond to him after their conversation on their journey. Hamilton heard her, throwing back his head and laughing louder.

"You aren't wrong. But come along and let me show you their few animals. Ransom isn't really a rancher. He just wanted a large piece of countryside to call his own. But he has some animals for their own use and a bit extra just in case."

Sadie laughed along with him and followed him to the barn. They took their time admiring the animals. Sadie couldn't help admiring the Delaneys' large home, as well. While she had fallen deeply in love with Hamilton's house on first sight, if she hadn't, she would probably be envious of Ransom and Hannah's beautiful home. The large house sparkled with its many windows.

Hamilton laughed when he saw the direction of Sadie's gaze. "Hannah always says it's obvious there's no tax on windows in Nebraska. Ransom seemed to want to flaunt that fact."

"I wonder how they got so very much glass here without breaking it. That must have been a feat in itself."

"It's not so very difficult. We managed to get plenty of glass to our property."

Sadie blushed, feeling as though she had been disloyal in her admiration of the other house. She was saved from her mortification by a new arrival.

"Hamilton Foster, as I live and breathe," boomed a loud voice from behind them, making Sadie jump.

She watched in fascination as the two large men shook hands and slapped each other on the back. It appeared almost painful to Sadie, but the two men seemed very happy to see one another.

"Allow me to introduce my wife, Sadie."

Her face filled with more color as the pleasure of being introduced in such a way flooded through her. While her husband seemed to wish her elsewhere, he wasn't going to deny her place in his life, at least not in front of others.

"It's a pleasure to meet you, Sadie. But what are you doing out here in the barn? Hannah will be thrilled to have you here. Do say you can stay for a few days."

Sadie waited quietly for Hamilton to answer. A part of her wanted to leave immediately, embarrassed to inconvenience these strangers. But the rest of her desperately wanted some new friends and yearned to learn more about her husband in the process.

Hamilton's gaze seemed to scour her face before he turned back toward Mr. Delaney. "To be honest, we arrived unannounced and were wondering if we ought not to stay considering Abigail is so sick."

"She's not all that sick, I don't think. Hannah is just a little frazzled with juggling the baby with the rest. Is that why you're out here?"

Sadie finally spoke up. "Hamilton was just giving me a tour in order to allow Hannah a few minutes to prepare a little."

Ransom's eyebrows rose. "I didn't realize he had such tact in him."

Hamilton laughed and thumped his friend on the back. "I don't. That's why I have a wife."

Ransom stepped closer to Sadie, taking her arm. "Well, we're honored to have you visit us, Sadie. You'll have your hands full with this one, I'm sure. Now, if I know my wife, she's probably standing at a window wondering what has become of all of us. Let's go in and have some tea."

Whether she was watching from a window or not, Sadie wasn't to know, but when they went in, Hannah was indeed ready for visitors.

"Welcome, welcome, I'm thrilled to have you here. Thank you for coming to visit us."

Sadie could smell something sweet baking in the oven and saw steam coming from the kettle. Their hostess had clearly been busy while they had been exploring in the barn. Sadie smiled her thanks to the other woman.

The evening passed quickly with the three friends catching up. Sadie enjoyed listening to them but had little to share herself. She also very much enjoyed getting to know Hannah's young brother and sister as well as Ransom's cute little niece. She was grateful the Delaneys didn't pry into her background beyond exclaiming over her friendship with Fredericksburgs. Before long, Sadie was surprised by a large yawn that she tried to stifle.

"Oh, silly me, I was so caught up with visiting that I haven't even shown you to your room. With your travels today, you must be very tired."

In that moment, Sadie realized the awkward situation they were about to encounter, and her gaze flew toward Hamilton. He frowned at her, and she made every effort to stifle her discomfort, simply following Hannah up the stairs to a nicely appointed guest room.

"This is the only room in the house that is somewhat unscathed by the children. I hope you'll be able to make yourself comfortable here. Please, let me know if you have need of anything at all."

"Thank you so much, Mrs. Delaney, you've been more than hospitable."

"Please, let's be friends. You must call me Hannah, and I will call you Sadie."

"I'd like that, thank you," Sadie answered quietly as her hostess slipped from the room, closing the door quietly behind her. Sadie was left standing in the middle of the room gripping her small satchel tightly, wondering what she ought to do with herself.

There was only one bed. It was quite a large bed. But since she had never shared a bed with her husband, she was beyond uncomfortable. Looking around the tidy room, Sadie wondered if she could make a spot for herself on the floor. After forcing her limbs from the temporarily paralyzed state, she discovered there were extra blankets in a trunk at the foot of the bed.

When Hamilton stepped into the room, he remained by the door and watched her pile the bedding into the corner of the room. Sadie could feel his steady gaze and wanted to squirm but managed to quell the impulse.

Finally stepping closer, Hamilton quietly said, "Thank you for making a bed for me."

Sadie recoiled. "This isn't for you. I wouldn't expect you to take the floor. I didn't mean to –" She stammered to a halt when he put his hand gently on her arm.

"I completely understand. Don't worry about it. I should have thought about this when I so impulsively decided to visit my friends. It wasn't well done of me on many counts."

Sadie opened her mouth to contradict him but nothing came out. She simply didn't know what to say.

"Go to sleep, Sadie. It has been a long day. I can see you worrying behind your small smile. I promise you, this will be far more comfortable than many of the times I've slept outdoors while out with the cattle. So, thank you for piling so many blankets down for me."

Sadie was struggling with what was best to do when she heard Hamilton's sigh. "Go to bed, Sadie. There's nothing to be gained from worrying about it now, I promise you. This isn't your fault. We both need to sleep." Without looking at her, he flipped back one of the blankets and lay down without removing any of his clothing. "Please, don't forget to blow out the candle before you get into bed."

Blinking at him, Sadie felt as though she were being remarkably dull-witted. There was nothing to be done. She couldn't argue with him over the bed. He was already lying down. She just needed to get on with the process of sleeping. It was nighttime, and she would need her energy the next day. There was nothing she could do but blow out the candle, crawl into bed, and hope for oblivion to claim her. She was tired enough after the long day in the buck wagon that she expected to fall instantly asleep.

It wasn't quite instantaneous. For one thing, except for the few times she had been unable to buy coal in the dead of winter, she had never slept in all her clothes. It was awkward to say the least. Finally, after struggling to find a comfortable position, she realized it was ridiculous and quietly removed her top layer of clothing. She would be covered by blankets and was wearing several layers. Besides, she was married to the man. If he saw her ankles, surely they would both survive the experience. The smile that accompanied that thought allowed her to relax enough to finally fall asleep. The next thing she knew, sunlight was pouring through the window. She had slept through the night.

The night before she had forgotten to draw the curtains, which was why the light had awoken her. It wasn't so very bright, so Sadie was assured that it wasn't very late. She could be downstairs helping their hostess before anyone even realized the awkward sleeping arrangements she and Hamilton had endured.

She shouldn't actually say endured, even in her mind. The bed had been exceptionally comfortable. Sadie really couldn't complain. She ought to feel sorry for Hamilton for taking the floor. But the fact that he was still asleep led her to believe that perhaps he wasn't so terribly uncomfortable. Or maybe, her conscience made her realize, he was still asleep because he had been too uncomfortable to sleep deeply until exhaustion finally pulled him under. That was far more likely.

Sadie tried to ignore her guilty conscience and hurried down the stairs.

Chapter Eight

Hamilton opened his eyes and stretched. As soon as he had heard Sadie rustling around he had frozen and feigned sleep, not wanting to make the poor woman even more uncomfortable than she already was. It had been nearly impossible to keep his breathing steady and his body still, as he felt her watchful gaze upon him while she debated what to do.

He had been relieved the night before when he had finally heard her settle into sleep. It had been strangely restful having another person in the room, not something he had expected at all. He hadn't shared a room since childhood, but despite how many secrets he was keeping from her, he found Sadie's company restful. Almost as soon as she had stopped fidgeting and fallen asleep, he had, too. And then he had slept deeper than he had since his wife had arrived in Nebraska.

Giving his head a shake, Hamilton climbed to his feet, stretching out the kinks in his muscles. While he hadn't lied when he told Sadie that the floor with all the blankets was slightly more comfortable than sleeping outdoors on the range, that wasn't really saying much. He liked his creature comforts and would look forward to returning home to his soft bed. But they would have to stay with Delaneys for at least one more night or his friends would take offence.

As it was, they stayed several nights, since Hannah and Sadie hit it off, as Hamilton had known they would. Sadie was happily making preserves and helping Hannah prepare for the coming winter. And they hadn't even caught whatever had been ailing Abigail, despite Sadie's worries.

"How do you know all these things?" Hamilton heard Hannah marveling. "You are so much better prepared for life out here than I ever was."

Sadie's tinkling laugh made Hamilton's breath catch, despite the conversation he was in with Ransom.

"Not all of us grew up with servants, Hannah," she had said without a trace of discomfort in her voice. Hamilton was surprised to hear them both dissolving into laughter before he was reabsorbed into his own conversation. He felt a catch in his throat as he was once again reminded that not all beautiful women were like his mother. He really ought to wrap his head around that and resolve his resistance toward his wife.

After the first night, Sadie had seemed to accept that he was going to sleep on the floor, but she piled more and more blankets into the creation of his bed each night. It had been a source of amusement for Hamilton each time he entered the room to see his bed appearing taller than the night before. He wasn't even sure how Sadie managed it so quickly as she was also always burrowed under her own covers by the time he entered the room, appearing to be fast asleep, which he knew was a ruse. He was relieved to note, though, that her breathing smoothed out into the rhythm of sleep within minutes of his entry to the room. If he were being fanciful he would almost think she found his presence comforting. At least his arrival didn't prevent her from sleep.

"My wife sure is enjoying your wife's company, Hamilton." Ransom's comment made Hamilton's chest puff up with pride. "She seems like a good woman. But you seem a bit off." The other man laughed when Hamilton scowled at him. "I know, I'm turning into a woman. But Hannah has taught me that feelings aren't the dreadful things I once thought they were. Do you want to talk about what's going on with you?"

"No, I do not," Hamilton sputtered.

Ransom slapped him on the back and chuckled. "That's good. I didn't really want to either, but I know enough to figure I ought to at least ask."

Hamilton allowed the moment to pass but he couldn't get it out of his mind the entire time they were visiting with Delaneys. While Sadie seemed to be thriving under the attention of a new friend, Hamilton watched and marveled. Ransom was right. His wife was a good woman. And he had been doing nothing but ignoring her just because she was beautiful like his mother. But Sadie was nothing like his mother had been. It was unfair of him to paint her with the same brush. Sadie had been loyal to her family and her debts. Hamilton could trust that she would be loyal to him. And he knew beyond any doubt that she would never leave a child of hers behind like his mother had. It had been foolish of him to judge her so harshly just because she was so pretty. He ought to have known that beauty was only skin deep. What Sadie had came from her core.

When Sadie had shown Hannah, Maryanne, and Francine how to make jam, Hannah had begged that they stay a few more days so they could learn even more things from Sadie. Hamilton had frowned over the wind he heard howling outside but reluctantly agreed to stay a little longer.

"We have to be mindful of the potential for a turn in the weather. But it shouldn't hurt to stay a little bit longer." When he had seen how happy Sadie seemed to be at the prospect of more days with the others, he was comfortable with his decision.

Despite the extra days, before he realized it, the visit had flown by and he found himself once more in the wagon with Sadie bundled up beside him, a contented smile upon her face.

"That was far more enjoyable than I expected it to be when we first arrived," she said, as they pulled around a corner and could no longer see the Delaneys waving to them from their front porch.

Hamilton laughed. "Me, too. I'm sorry for bringing you into such an awkward situation. It was certainly not my intention when we set out for this visit."

"Of course, not," Sadie agreed promptly. "Who in their right mind would go looking for awkwardness?"

Hamilton laughed. "But you did enjoy the visit, didn't you?"

"Very much so," Sadie agreed immediately before adding with an impish smile, "Although I will now have to keep our house always in readiness for guests, as they assured us they would visit us in turn. I'm sure they'll be arriving without warning just as we did."

"I'm not so sure. They are a much more cumbersome package being a family of six. They aren't likely to set out without full assurance that we'll be ready for them."

Sadie hummed. Hamilton wasn't sure if it was in agreement or not so he didn't pursue the matter. He was happy to allow silence to rise up between them. It wasn't the uncomfortable quiet that had kept them company on the drive there. At least, not at first. But then, after a mile or two he realized Sadie was deep in troubled thoughts.

"Are you worrying again?" he asked with a chuckle.

She shrugged, clearly not wanting to discuss her thoughts with him. But a few moments later she surprised him with her question.

"When will you be leaving for California?"

"I beg your pardon?" Hamilton was shocked. He had heard her clearly but couldn't wrap his mind around her words. He had never mentioned California to her before.

"Hannah told me how lucky I am that your other businesses are in California instead of Oregon like Ransom's. She was concerned, though, that the vastness of your empire might require a great deal of your time, and you might get stuck there for the winter, since you haven't left yet on your usual trip to check on things."

Hamilton wanted to curse out his frustrations but managed to contain his anger, not even transferring his thoughts to the horses via the reins. But it was a struggle.

"What else did she say?" He tried to sound merely interested, but his feelings must have conveyed themselves to her. Despite the fact that she seemed upset with him, she now looked concerned over his rising anger.

Sadie shrugged. "She didn't say much else aside from mentioning that she was surprised you had gotten married, as she suspected you might not want children due to your anger towards your own mother. I think she felt bad for embarrassing me with the fact that she knew so much more about your circumstances than I do."

"I've been friends with Ransom for ten years. He's obviously told her things."

A bitter laugh came from the sweet woman beside him. It sounded strange coming from her. "Yes, I've heard some husbands do that."

He deserved her sarcasm, even if it sat oddly on her.

"I'd like to walk for a while, please."

"No, Sadie, it's too cold," he protested.

"Walking will warm me up, I'm sure," she insisted.

"It's a bad idea, Sadie. But if you really insist, the horses are about due for a rest. You can walk a ways ahead of us while I let them have a little break. I'll catch up to you. Hopefully you'll be ready to see reason by then." Hamilton was angry that she was kicking up a fuss about what he hadn't told her, so he didn't ague any further with her, merely watching silently as she started walking down the road without a backward glance.

~~~

Sadie stomped along beside the road, her anger and disappointment chasing each other around in her mind while her puffs of breath created clouds in the cold air in front of her face. Within minutes, her nose and cheeks became chilled and she became aware of the darkening sky. She was being ridiculous. Hamilton hadn't lied to her. She had never thought to ask him about other businesses. The fact that he hadn't volunteered the information meant he was private, not necessarily a liar. And as they had frequently admitted to each other, they were still getting to know each other. Strangers, even though Sadie hadn't considered him a stranger since the first week.

It wasn't Hamilton's fault that she had allowed her heart to become involved. She hadn't meant to. Sadie had tried to remain aloof from him, refusing to acknowledge that she was growing to care for him. But whether she admitted it or not, her heart wasn't meant for a solitary existence. She had grown fond of her husband. Maybe even more than fond. Which was probably why she had been so deeply embarrassed to realize he had kept such big secrets from her. She had told him every detail of her life, and he hadn't trusted her with his own.

Her humiliation had made her angry. And now, here she was walking down a dirt road in the middle of Nebraska with no real idea of where she was and not a single living soul within sight or earshot. Sadie admitted to herself that she was a fool. She only hoped Hamilton didn't stay angry with her and would come along to collect her before too much longer.

She walked and walked. It felt like she was walking for hours, but she had no way to really judge. The sky had grown darker, and now flakes of snow were swirling in the cold air and accumulating on the road in front of her. It wasn't too hard to walk yet, but she was growing more and more concerned. She would have thought Hamilton would have reached her long ago. The horses wouldn't have needed to rest for very long. It wasn't as though the wagon was laden down with heavy burdens. Surely her husband's anger wouldn't have made him dally and leave her walking alone longer than necessary. Not that it was necessary, Sadie reminded herself. She was the one who had stomped off on her own into the great yonder.

Her heart constricted as she realized the truth. Somehow she had gotten herself lost. In the middle of Nebraska. In an early snowstorm. And she knew nothing about survival.

That's not true, she told herself. You know plenty about survival. You've survived all that life has thrown you up until now, surely you can figure out a little bit of cold and snow.

The encouraging thoughts bolstered her courage for a while, but soon she was dragging her feet once more. She didn't know if she ought to keep walking or if she should try to build herself some sort of nest in the snow. Sadie had once read a book about how animals did that to survive the harsh weather. If it worked for the animals, surely it would work for her.

~~~

Hamilton was going hoarse from yelling Sadie's name. Fear had him firmly in its grip. He was the worst sort of fool for having allowed her to walk off on her own. He had lost her. In a snowstorm. He was frantic with worry, and there was no way of getting help. From what he recalled, the next village was several miles away. And with the gathering darkness, if he didn't find her soon, getting others wasn't going to be of any help to his wife if she was a frozen block of ice.

He had retraced his route several times after following along the route she had surely taken. He couldn't understand how he could have missed her. She must have taken the wrong turn somewhere along the way.

Hamilton carefully turned the wagon around and set off quickly to where the roads diverged, following the wrong road, hoping desperately it would end up being the right one.

A couple miles further and his heart was starting to sink. It had been hours. This section of wilderness expanded in all directions for miles with barely a soul stirring at the best of times, let alone during a snowstorm.

He was just about to give up and turn around to find another road she might have chosen when he caught sight of a splash of color. It was almost the same color as the coat she had been wearing. Before he had even brought the horses to a standstill he was on the ground and running forward.

"Sadie," he called to her as he pulled her up from the ground. "Sadie, my darling girl, wake up. Are you hurt? Wake up and tell me. I swear to you, I'll never let you out of my sight ever again."

He almost wept with relief when he realized she was still breathing, but her skin was so white it was the color of the snow that was continuing to fall around them. He needed to get her to warmth. Staring in the direction she had been facing, he realized the young woman wasn't a total fool. There was a rather ramshackle barn off in the distance.

Hamilton quickly unhitched the horses, laying Sadie over one of them and covering her with the furs from the wagon before leading them all in the direction of the dilapidated building.

Once there, he was relieved to see there was some old straw that he was able to divide — some to feed the horses and some more to create a cocoon of sorts for himself and his wife.

He managed to wrestle Sadie out of her soaked overcoat, relieved to realize that she wasn't wet all the way through. If he'd had to, he would have lit a fire, but Hamilton was afraid he would end up burning down their only source of protection from the storm.

"Sadie, wake up, sweet thing. I need you to try to open your eyes." At her soft moan, Hamilton redoubled his efforts to wake her up, relieved to have some signs of life. "Come on, Sadie. I know you want to sleep, but you need to talk to me. I don't want to take your clothes off to examine you for injury if I don't have to." Despite his fears, he had to chuckle over the fact that his words finally prompted a reaction out of her. She groaned a little bit but finally her eyes fluttered open. When her gaze seemed to finally focus on him, he was amazed to see a soft smile stretch her face.

"Hello there," he said to her. "I was getting mightily worried about you."

Tears filled her eyes, one tipping over the edge of her lashes, and he quickly wiped it away. "So sorry, Ham, didn't mean to be an idiot," she mumbled. He smiled over her use of his shortened name, but he quickly corrected her.

"I'm the idiot, not you. I never should have allowed you to get out of the wagon. It was foolish beyond forgiveness at the best of times, but I should have realized that the weather was going to take a turn."

Her chattering teeth prevented her from saying too much more, but Hamilton was relieved to see her gaze was clearing. He didn't think she had hit her head.

"Did you slip and fall? I found you lying prone in the snow."

"So cold," she said, making Hamilton wonder if she was talking about now or then. He pulled her tighter into his side, willing his own heat to warm her. "So lost," she added. "Tried to get to the barn but slipped. Was going to just rest for a minute to catch my breath." She sounded breathless as she said it, and Hamilton's heart constricted at the risk they had run. He was lucky he had found her when he had. A little bit longer, and she would have been covered by the falling snow. He squeezed her tightly to him, surprising a gasp of laughter out of her. "Still need my breath," she added.

He chuckled, too, but didn't loosen his grasp by much. "I was never so happy nor so angry all at once in my life," he said as he stared into her face and dropped a light kiss onto the tip of her nose. She blinked slowly at him, and her brow furrowed into confusion.

"Am I dreaming?" she asked.

"No, my darling, I've got you. We're safe, and dry, and somewhat warm. We've got the horses and some straw, and we'll be all right here until morning when we'll make our way home. To our house that you are making into a home for us. And I swear to you, I'll tell you all my secrets. It just might take some time to get them all out." She offered him a drowsy smile, and Hamilton wasn't sure if she even fully understood what he was saying. But he couldn't hold back. "The first secret I have to tell you is that I love you."

Her eyes had drifted closed, but they popped open as his words seemed to register. Her gaze was more alert and her smile was shy but more lively than before.

"Really?"

"Really! I swear to you, I'll never keep anything from you again, nor will I ever let anything bad happen to you."

Sadie shrugged, but happiness started to shine through her features. "Bad things happen," she said in a soft voice. "But I love you, too." She paused for a moment. "And I'll try not to be ridiculous in the future."

Hamilton held her close, grateful they had survived. He had come so close to losing the beautiful future he now saw unfurling before them.

Epilogue

S adie stood on the edge of the porch watching the lane. She knew she was being foolish. It was doubtful the Delaneys would have left their house at six o'clock in the morning, so they couldn't possibly be arriving yet. But she was anxious for them to get there.

It was going to be a perfect summer day. The children were finished with school, so it was good timing for the family of six to come for a visit. The telegram had arrived the week before.

THOUGHT ABOUT SURPRISING YOU BUT DECIDED TO ADVISE YOU SIX TO ARRIVE NEXT WEEK TUESDAY

Sadie and Hamilton had laughed long and hard over the message before Sadie swept into a fervor of preparations, much to Hamilton's dismay.

"Shouldn't you be taking it more gently, in your condition?"

Shooting him a playfully exasperated glance, Sadie had answered, "I'm pregnant, not dying."

Hamilton had laughed but added, "I'd like to keep it that way. Here, let me do that," he had offered as he grabbed the mop from her hands and finished the task.

"Thank you. And I'm glad you're getting practice. You can't even tell I'm carrying yet, but in a few months,

I'll truly need your help with this type of task. For now, while I promise you I won't do too much, the doctor said there's nothing wrong with me continuing to do my usual activities."

"Well, preparing for six visitors isn't your usual activities," Hamilton had replied stubbornly. "We should have told them to stay away."

"No, we shouldn't have," Sadie countered with a firm shake of her head. "Stop worrying. Women have been bearing children since the beginning of time. There is no reason to expect anything to go wrong. And certainly doing a few house chores isn't going to do me any harm at this point."

Hamilton joined her on the porch, interrupting her musing.

"Hello beautiful."

Sadie grinned at him. The endearment was significant considering his strange feelings about physical beauty. Hamilton had come a long way in the short time they'd been together. It was hard to believe they'd only been married nine months. She felt like she'd known him for a lifetime.

"I know you're excited about them coming, but shouldn't you be sitting down?"

"Hamilton Foster, we've been over this. I am not going to wrap myself in cotton wool for the next six months."

Hamilton sighed. "Six months. It's such terrible timing, though. You'll be giving birth in the dead of winter."

Sadie grinned as she sidled up to him, draping her arms around his middle as his automatically came around and pulled her closer into his side. "Maybe that will be a good time to show me all your California properties, then. I've heard they don't get winter there."

His arms tightened around her while he shuffled her around to be more comfortable in front of him, and his chin dropped down onto her head. Sadie sighed contentedly, the sense of home-coming settling over her like a warm blanket.

"Some of my places there do get winter, some don't. Maybe that would be a good idea. Although I thought you would prefer to be here. You seem to be a nester."

Sadie giggled. "I never knew that about myself, but you're right. I really do like being home. But I enjoyed it when we took advantage of the early thaw and you took me to California in February and showed me some of your places. It's hard to believe the train actually goes all the way from coast to coast now. But, you're right. I *would* rather be here when the baby comes. Not to compare myself with the animals, but you've helped them give birth. Don't you think you will be able to help me?"

Even though she couldn't see his face, she could imagine him paling at the thought when she heard his breathing change. She tightened her arms around him, pulling her head out from under his chin so she could look into his face, accepting his light kiss as she did so.

"Ham, my darling, stop worrying. I know it's motivated by loving concern, but you're going to drive us both batty before the baby even gets here. We'll need all our mental faculties fully intact to cope with his or her arrival, so stop borrowing trouble. It's a perfect day, our friends are coming to visit, we're perfectly happy and healthy and in love. Nothing could be better than this."

His smile nearly took her breath away as he dropped another kiss onto her upturned face. "You're right. I promise to try a bit harder to stop worrying. But since, as you know, my mother left when I was only eight, I have very little experience with female issues. And delivering my own child is not something I want to experience, as I am absolutely certain it will not be the same thing as a colt or calf."

Sadie grinned up at him. "You're probably right. We could hire a nurse to come and stay with us. Since you're the one who's so worried about it, it might be a good way for you to spend a bit of that abundance of money you didn't want to tell me about."

Hamilton's chuckle rumbled through her making her shiver with delight as her smile widened. "Are you ever going to forget about my previous secretive nature?"

"Eventually," Sadie answered after a slight pause. "It'll be easy to forget about since you seem to have made such a complete turnabout. I mean, I bet you would even let me count your gold if I was so inclined."

"Of course, I would," Hamilton replied, his tone a mixture of affront and amusement. "It just might take you a while."

Sadie laughed while she tightened her arms around his waist. "I'm glad you've grown comfortable telling me about your different businesses and investments. I find it fascinating even if I don't fully understand how some of it works. You'll probably have to explain the borax process at least one or two times more before I could speak intelligently on the matter."

Hamilton loyally countered her words. "You can speak intelligently on any matter, since you're far smarter than anyone would think from looking at you."

Sadie couldn't prevent her burst of laughter in response before she sighed. "Hamilton, you're going to have to come to terms with the fact that your mother's beauty had nothing to do with her faithlessness." She tightened her arms to prevent him from pulling away. "I still think you ought to try to find her so you could confront her. You've only ever heard your father's side of the story. Since you were so young, you can't really trust your own recollections. I can assure you, I'm far from the only trustworthy woman on earth. While you'll never have to worry about finding another wife, you still ought to work on your views as we will want to make friends with people. Especially with a child on the way. I'll need to know the other mothers when he or she goes to school, at the very least."

"Well, none of the women around here are very pretty, so it's not much of an issue." He chuckled and dropped another gentle kiss to her lips while squeezing her back when he realized she was about to protest. "I know. You're right about my mother. I shouldn't have judged all other women on her bad behavior."

Sadie's frown prompted a sigh from Hamilton. "Maybe you're right. Maybe I don't even know if her behavior was so very bad. But I do know that you would never leave your child behind, no matter the circumstances."

Hamilton was quiet for a moment, looking out over his land, which always seemed to bring pleasure to his troubled soul. Sadie didn't interrupt his process, content knowing he was making an effort to alter his thoughts.

"I will consider hiring someone to look for her," he said in a tired voice before his tone lightened. "But in the meantime," he continued, keeping his gaze on the horizon. "I love you, I'm thrilled to have you, even if you're so pretty it hurts my eyes sometimes. More importantly, I trust you, and if that small cloud of dust over there means what I think it does, our friends are going to be here in the next ten or fifteen minutes."

The first part of his speech had made Sadie feel swoony with the depth of her own love for her handsome husband, but the rest of his words made her pull out of his arms with a little jump of agitated joy as she pulled off her apron and reached up to feel if any of her hairs were out of place.

"Sadie." His tone was a little sharper than he had maybe meant it to be as she brought a slightly startled gaze to his face. "You look perfect, the house is ready, you've cooked and baked until the house is overflowing, and you're with child so you shouldn't be overly excited anyway."

With a happy gurgle of laughter, Sadie threw herself back into her husband's arms. "I love you, Hamilton Foster. I'm looking forward to the rest of our lives together." Then she stood on the tips of her toes and stifled any more of his worries with the gentle pressure of her warm lips.

The End

About the Author

I've been writing pretty much since I learned to read when I was five years old. Of course, those early efforts were basically only something a mother could love :-). I put writing aside after I left school and stuck with reading. I am an avid reader. I love words. I will read anything, even the cereal box, signs, posters, etc. But my true love is novels.

Almost ten years ago my husband dared me to write a book instead of always reading them. I didn't think I'd be able to do it, but to my surprise I love writing. Those early efforts eventually became my first published book – Tempting the Earl (published by Avalon Books in 2010). There were some ups and downs in my publishing efforts. My first publisher was sold and I became an "orphan" author, back to the drawing board of trying to find a publishing house. It has been a thrilling adventure as I learned to navigate the world of publishing.

I believe firmly that everyone deserves a happily ever after. I want my readers to be able to escape from the everyday for a little while and feel upbeat and refreshed when they get to the end of my books.

When not reading or writing, I can be found traipsing around my neighborhood admiring the dogs and greenery or travelling the world with my favorite companion.

Stay in touch:

Website - sign up for my newsletter:
www.wendymayandrews.com

Facebook -
facebook.com/groups/WMASweetRomanceReadersAndFriends

Instagram - www.instagram.com/WendyMayAndrews

Twitter - www.twitter.com/WendyMayAndrews

Other books by Wendy May Andrews you will enjoy:

Another American Historical, read:

Book 1 in the Orphan Train series:

Sophie

She'd happily give him her heart ... if only it wouldn't cost her the only home she's known

Sophie Brooks thought she had everything she could want in life. Friends, loved ones at the orphanage where she was raised, a job that gives her purpose, and a chance to help children every day ... what more could she need? But a chance encounter with a handsome stranger has her wondering if a life—and love—outside the orphanage might be exactly what she never knew she needed.

Renton Robert Rexford III has never wanted for anything. Until he meets Sophie. The charming, intelligent beauty draws him like no other. But, thanks to a disapproving benefactor who threatens to pull the orphanage's funding, his pursuit of her could cost Sophie everything she holds dear. She's all he wants in the world, but how can he ask her to give up so much when all she'd get in return is his heart?

It's not long before Sophie is forced to weigh her loyalty to the only home she's ever known against the needs of her heart. Can love prevail—or is the cost simply too high?

Available now on Amazon

If you like Regency Romance, read

Inheriting Trouble

Book 1 in the Bequest Series

The inheritance was meant to better her life, not muddle it.

Georgia Holton, wellborn but nearly penniless, is best friends with one of the Earl of Sherton's five daughters. When she is invited to accompany her friend for two weeks of the Season, Georgia jumps at the opportunity to have a little adventure away from her small village.

The Earl of Crossley is handsome, wealthy, widowed, and jaded. He has no intention of courting any of this Season's debutantes. After all, every woman he's ever known has been dishonest, including his late wife. But when a chance encounter throws him into contact with the Sherton ladies and their lovely friend, he can't help being drawn to Georgia's beauty and endearing personality.

When confusion about Georgia's small inheritance becomes known, a sense of obligation to right a wrong forces the earl and Georgia into close association.

But is she really different from any of the other women, or does she have an ulterior motive?

And can Georgia even consider getting close to a man from High Society, when all she wants is to return to her simple village life?

Sparks fly between these two, but it will take forgiveness and understanding on both their parts to reach a happily ever after.

Available now on Amazon

If you like Regencies with a touch of adventure, you will love

the Mayfair Mayhem series. Book 1 is:

The Duke Conspiracy

**Anything is possible with a spying debutante,
a duke, and a conspiracy.**

Growing up, Rose and Alex were the best of friends until their families became embroiled in a feud. Now, the Season is throwing them into each other's company. Despite the spark of attraction they might feel for one another, they each want very different things in life, besides needing to support their own family's side in the dispute.

Miss Rosamund Smythe is finding the Season to be a dead bore after spying with her father, a baron diplomat, in Vienna. She wants more out of life than just being some nobleman's wife. When she overhears a plot to entrap Alex into a marriage of convenience, her intrigue and some last vestige of loyalty causes them to overcome the feud.

His Grace, Alexander Milton, the Duke of Wrentham, wants a quiet life with a "proper" wife after his tumultuous childhood. His parents had fought viciously, lied often, and Alex had hated it all.

Rose's meddling puts her in danger. Alex will have to leave the simple peace he craves to claim a love he never could have imagined. Can they claim their happily ever after despite the turmoil?

Available now on <u>Amazon</u>

Made in the USA
Monee, IL
29 October 2022